MW00635730

Trenches

A journal in the mind of a young black man living in Baltimore, Maryland

Charles Mays

Table of Contents

Block Boys

Not one for the trouble that being black attracts, Robert Peters is the average, well not so average black male growing up on the East side of Baltimore. He has both parents, the latter which is unordinary. The black community is stereotyped as only broken homes filled with broken men & women. The Media portrays African Americans as animals who statistically will never go anywhere except through the criminal justice system, & government assistance.

Robert is a caramel complexion almost average height male with a slim build. His hair is fair & short. His eyes are narrow as if in a perpetual state of exhaustion. He has a wide bridged nose with large lips that gives him a defining quiet look.

Marlon is almost the opposite, although younger, he is average height, around 5ft8 & dark-skinned. Marlon has a slim build but defined abs & shoulder bones. His lips are large as well, but his eyes are wide & attentive. He has a defining scar on his left cheek from when a Rottweiler jumped up & got a piece of his face.

For Robert, the strangest thing to him is being born with a pure heart in such a corrupt environment. Pure in the sense that his presence in his neighborhood made him more of a martyr, or an outcast rather.

These transgressions define siblings Robert & Marlon's lives' in two distinctively different ways.

Red and blue lights flash

Robert & Marlon patiently sit on the front of the entrance to the corner Lafayette house.

"Stand up" bellows the first African American officer. "Anything in your pockets? What are y'all up to?"

"For what?! We live here!" Yells Marlon. "These are our steps. We're just chilling after hooping at school, soaking in the sunset."

Marlon is my defensive younger brother. He can never hide his disgust whenever black cops profile us. At least he could understand white cops, they have no clue what makes a black man. The black cops however, one would expect some form of commonality.

"Show me your Id's." He continues to profile.

We quickly reveal our permits to the Baltimore cop, both sharing unsympathetic glances & inside grief as we comply with the orders.

"Here, it says we live at 1300 East Lafayette Avenue." Marlon proudly exclaims. The officer "flash-lit" our id's as the sun was at its peak of descent.

"Aight everything checks out. I hope you fellas know that we aren't out here just harassing you because we feel like it." The officer replies while holding the still holstered butt of his gun.
As soon as we get our id's back, another batch of officers pull up & ask for the same things, this time a lot less nice.

"Ay get up! What's in your pockets?" The second African American cop demands.

"Nah, nah, they good they live here I checked them out." The first officer defends.

"My bad shordy." Officer number 2 apologizes.

"It is what it is," I reply while watching the other boys sitting on old lady Gloria's steps across the street. They dip around her corner house while the cops occupy our time. They narrowly avoid any attention because it is diverted to Marlon & me which is another gripe Marlon has with the police. They didn't do any due diligence even checking the address they were called to.

"Gloria must have complained about those boys sitting on her steps" I continue.

We aren't accepted by the other guys in our neighborhood. We go to school, don't smoke, are grounded & rooted in church but what is surprising to them, is that we have a father in our lives. Even if he is a detached one.

"So, are you guys in school?" Asks officer number 2.

"Yes sir" both Marlon & I exclaim proudly.
"We both attend the University of Baltimore" we answer simultaneously sounding as if twins.

That is what everyone in the hood calls us anyways.
While we converse with the first two cops, a patty wagon pulls up alongside our house from which the driver steps out in all of his stereotypical glory.

"These the niggas that were on the lady steps?" He asks. "Always some young ass niggas. Y'all have any warrants? They have probably been arrested, let me see your id's Imma run them through the system."

"They all good man, they live here. Relax."

"You should have still run their shit. This a public assistance joint, or lead check, cause this a pretty big house? I'm just fucking wit y'all. Aight bro Imma get up with y'all, I'm bout to scoop the junkie from North Ave at the bar they just called it in. Somebody hit his ass & he ran to the bar trying to get behind the counter."

"Man, you crazy, chill out. We're finished here just chatting up with them a bit." Replies the first officer.

"Don't waste too much time with them muthafuckas." Officer number 3 exclaims as he proceeds to re-enter the white patty wagon with his potbelly caressing the steering wheel.

What I hate the most about the hood is that the enemies are not the ones I read in textbooks, but people of my complexion. The guys around here are black just as we are, & yet still there is no common ground. The cops are even worse. Judging from behind a badge.
I wonder sometimes why God even created these circumstances for me to deal with in the first place. How come there is a man of authority that looks like me but won't love me the same as his kin?
Instead I am taught about the white man's oppression. Yet I feel like the very people who will shoot me dead are the ones with the peanut butter faces. Well I suppose I am more focused on physical oppression than systematic. In any case, I have to make it out of the hood to be able to experience systematic abuse.

I find it amusing that I am looking forward to being abused systematically but not as excited at the prospect of success. As a black man, I am already trained to see the negatives.
Oh, how the mind works wonders in a single instant. The speck of time over this mind-boggling realization has me daydreaming.

"We're not all like that, just like you guys aren't all like the rest of the kids around here. Stay humble & stay in school. Have each-others backs, because coming from here, no one will give you handouts, so don't expect any."

That conversation about how we are different continues for quite some time, which only infuriates the local neighborhood "thugs" & wannabe "typical urban superstars". It does not matter to us though, because we stay to ourselves & watch each other's backs.

The cops proceeded to take off in their separate squad cars after fraternizing with one another.
The neighborhood boys mug us from across the basketball court. It is an alpha male sort of thing to them, something Marlon & I do not care to participate in.

"What's funny to me is that we are all in the hood, & we are all struggling the same way. We all like nice shoes, chicks, & hooping. So what's the problem?" Marlon asks.

"Got to look at it from their point of view. They trying to fuck everything that moves but never had a father to even teach them how." I joke.

Well at least that is how my parents justify the disdain of us.

Trenches

A typical day sitting on the stoop on Lafayette. We watch the unknown cars roll pass & keep on chit-chatting about our predicament of being black in the trenches of Baltimore.

Trenches

My Dawg

"Dimes on the reddy! Unknown coming down Aiken!" That is just a few of the drug selling signals that I am familiar with.

"Man it's hot out here." Says Rico "...& I'm not talking about the weather ya dig?"

"Ha-ha. Shit hey, they gotta get it someway my nigga no one is going give any of these guys a real shot in the real world. Have you ever attempted to build a resume? And sit waiting on someone to call you just to tell you that you are under qualified?" I ask.

"Thanks George bush! Shit the way this economy fucked up I'm bout to start slinging too you feel me?" Rico brags.

"Either that or go trick down Baltimore street." I laugh.

"Fucking faggot!" Rico screams.

Baltimore Street or "baudimo" Street as Baltimoreans pronounce it, is a street in the heart of downtown known for all of its strip clubs along with women & some men parading in women's clothing. Each individual attempts to sell themselves for dough.

What they did with the money is strictly their business according to my dad.

"Trying hoop?" Rico asks.

"Sure, why not I got time to bust that ass hahaha."

The basketball court is parallel to my house. It is a gift & a curse to have a corner house. One could not imagine the many times a basketball, or football has smashed in our windows.
My parents shelter Marlon & I from the basketball court because it is deemed unsafe. If the knockers come looking for the dope boys, the dope boys will just pretend to play basketball & on numerous occasions it works. The only time I really get to play is when my parents are not lurking.

"Uh, two-four!!" Rico parades as he drives to the basket. "Shit my shot wet nigga, plus you can't stick me cause I blow right past you, better play defense!"

"Nigga you hack every time you get to the basket, fuck outta here!" I defend.

"Call it! Stop being a bitch & call the foul. This is street-ball I'm not giving you shit so make sure you call it like I called your sister last night!" Rico teases.

"Chill hold on, hold on, time out! All that other shit irrelevant dug I'm here to play ball. " I reply out of breath.

I take advantage of that flurry of insults just to get my second wind. My stamina is not as great as it was when I was younger & in better shape. I am still fairly young & skinny, but you could not prove it to my lungs.

"I see you. You don't think I figured it out huh? Messing with them basic chicks got a nigga weak? Better stop giving them bitches a hundred percent dick my nigga." Rico baits. "Hahaha let me stop fucking with you. Point. How you want it?"

"Hard or soft?" I reply singing along with the Young Jeezy lyrics.

"Nigga I put you on fuck outta here" I brag, knowing that it was someone who put me on in the first place, which made me, in turn, put Rico on.

Rico is a neighborhood kid & my good friend. He wants to be part of the in-crowd which I feel is undesirable. I rather remain different & continue to be a nerd. I am quite fond of my sheltered life. It has made me socially awkward at times, yet it allows my imagination to run rampant. I guess that is a fair trade-off.

Rico lives close, within walking distance of my house, yet it takes him forever to get an outfit together because he is self-conscious of what the other neighborhood guys will think of him.

Rico's self-perception in relation to other people is pathetic. He needs not to compete with individuals who look at him as no more than a token nigga. He is an extra player in the video game that no one ever picks, yet somehow my weird ass will always pick him. It is safe to say Rico is my closest homie. I'd kill for Rico or for Marlon, though I hope that I will never have to. That I am confident about.

"Wanna see something dope?" Rico asks.

"Sure, I'm down."

We walk from the basketball court where I lost 13 to 7 back to my house entering through the back door.

We head in the dining room to get Rico's bag & then head to my room. It disgusts me because the entire time, Rico smiles profusely as if he beat me for some money or just won the lottery.
We arrive at my room up the stairs where Rico hollers, "aight shut the door", which I comply with. Rico proceeds to pull a "9x19" mm Walter p99 semiautomatic handgun from his bag. Don't ask me how I know what it is, I am probably wrong. I made a decent guess because when we first moved into this house, my oldest sister found a handgun that appeared pretty similar to the one Rico brandishes.

My parents ended up relinquishing the gun to my grandfather. He is a firearms enthusiast who can describe handguns with unique precision. The gun was found under a mattress in the basement's extra room. I can only fathom the many stories or instances where that gun was wielded or who were victimized by it.

Immediately my hands elevate. "Yo what the fuck are you doing?" I panic. "You gotta get that thing outta here!"

"Yo relax I found it behind Miss Peggy's store."

Miss Peggy is the candy store lady. She always "gyps" kids out of correct change because in her crude cruel words, "they didn't know better to learn how to count."

"We not going get caught because it ain't registered to nobody, look the serial number scratched," Rico says.

"Well I don't play with burners nigga. You gotta toss that bitch where you found it. Wipe off the prints. Anything but more importantly you can't be in here with that. I thought you were about to show me a new bittie you were hitting, not a damn ratchet!"

"Man, fuck that I got the heat dummy. This shit right here is what's happening all season. I wish a nigga would try me. Fuck around & smoke me a nigga this summer." Rico smiles. "Man stop being a bitch!"

"Nigga keep it down before somebody hears you."

"Man ain't nobody even here. You still scared look hold it?" Rico asks.

"Nah dug, that's all you," I reply with a trembling voice.

"Man stop being a pussy!" Rico says as he throws the gun in my lap. I jump & drop the heavy chunk of metal onto the floor.

"That thing could have gone off stupid!" I rage.

"Man, it's empty" Rico says as he bends down to pick it up. He aims it at different pictures pinned up on the walls around my dull room.

The pictures add flavor to my dreary room. The wooden outer panel layer is an eye-sore, so it's no wonder I have a million posters. A bunch of anime posters, along with scantily clad black women all over the place. Suffice to say I am a geek with flavor. Digimon & Bionicle posters plague the wall nearest my bed. If any real women ever smell a scent of immaturity on me, it will be a correct assumption.

At that moment the front door handle rattles & with a bang the door swings shut. I feel the air being sucked out of the house. Rico freaks & discharges the pistol into my chest.

BOOOOM!!!!!!

"Oh shit I didn't know it was anything in the chamber. I gotta get the fuck outta here."

Marlon rushes upstairs amidst the chaos.

"What the fuck are you doing?!" Marlon screams as he pushes Rico onto my twin mattress bed.

"I. I. I." Rico stutters. " I ain't know it was something in the chamber. I. Gotta."

My eyes begin to dim & my short life flashed before me. Marlon & Rico's visage faint from my sight. Choking on saliva, I lose consciousness while the reaper waits on my revival or my doom.

"Every niggas' fear, getting shot in the fucking hood."

"Call 911!"

Trenches

Transgressions

"Nine, one, one, What's your emergency?" "Uhm, there's been a shooting, please hurry, I'm just getting in, & I found my brother bleeding on the floor! We need..."

"Ok sir, keep calm, I am dispatching emergency services. Put pressure on the wound & keep him conscious. Do not move him unnecessarily. Don't touch anything else though, they should be there soon."

**Drip, Drip, Drip **

The iv drips in the room as Robby arouses.

My parents worry intensely waiting for answers. According to Marlon, I asked him to cover for Rico before I fainted a second time. If my dad discovers Rico is involved, that yellow tape on our doorsteps will be wrapped around his neck. Rico never caught favor from my father.

Just what our family needs, more cops at our doorsteps. Doorsteps they pay the mortgage on. Doorsteps they have kicked drug dealers off of. I can only imagine what is going through my folks' minds when they received the call. The main thought in mind is protecting Rico... my only friend. I mean what else can I say. Oh, that Rico shot me on accident. No! He is my best friend...my best friend that has my black ass in this uncomfortable hospital bed.

"Mr. & Mrs. Peters, your son was shot in pretty close proximity, luckily it's a non-fatal wound. There's an exit wound which typically indicates that the bullet traveled in one direction & exited Robert's back."

"Thanks doctor Deralock" replies Robert Sr.

Robert Sr. is a burly man, who stands at about 6 feet. A man with many trades & experiences. A man with plenty of integrity. Most fathers in his position escape their sons & daughters' lives, but not him. He begged his wife to keep me. Abortion was not an option & neither was abandoning us. By the next year After I was born, Marlon came miraculously. Our moms' tubes were tied after me.

It is funny that his refusal to be a deadbeat is one of the reasons we are outcast by our community in the neighborhood. The irony.

"Now Mr. Peters, the cops are going to want to know if your son or sons have any enemies." Dr. Deralock responds while focusing his eyes above his bi-focal glasses. He speedily exits the white & powder blue room to get an update & in his absence arrives detective Latham.

"Thank you, God," Mumbles Robert Sr.

"How are you folks holding up?" He greets. "My name is detective George Latham I'm from Baltimore city's homicide police unit." He continues.

"Homicide unit? But it wasn't a homicide it was an attempted armed robbery, right? A home invasion? Robert was just in the wrong place at the wrong time." Mrs. Peters asks.

Angie Peters is my mother, & a very blunt woman. Blunt & religious might I add. She's a vibrant woman, small, & brown skin. In her late thirties & not a trace of grey hair nor physically slowing down.

"Well typically we do come out for gun-related occurrences, but that's not the reason why. The circumstances surrounding your son's injury are sketchy." Replies detective Latham.

"Sketchy as in?"

"Well for starters, no forced entry, & no signs of a struggle. There's nothing that appears missing according to your list of valuables."

"That does seem strange," Angie replies.

"It's possible that whoever invaded your home was spooked by Robert & got away with nothing...But that's just an assumption. What we also know is that the same bullet that your son was shot with matches the same gun used to gun down a man in your neighborhood last month."

"Are you talking about Mr. Stevens?" Asks Robert Sr.

"Precisely, we haven't had a break in this case until now. With this new evidence we could be looking at the same guy. So, when he's done here, we will need him for further questioning with your approval & cooperation of course."

"Is he a suspect? He's a good kid, I'm positive that he has nothing to do with that murder." Asks Angie in the most saint way she possibly can.

"Again, no speculations at this point. Right now, your Robert is a victim." Replies the stocky well-dressed detective. "We're going to continue to play this by ear."

Trenches

Post dramatic stress

The police could not place a suspect, or Rico rather, in our house at the time I was shot. Rico's been in our house countless times, so his DNA wouldn't be out of the ordinary there. Of course, the suspicious detective has my parents not believing the hype in my recollection of what transpired, but what else do they have to go on?

I was shot without remembering any of what happened which is my story. I am sticking to it. My folks keep questioning my alibi, but it never changes.

"I was hooping, went upstairs to cool off & next thing I know, Marlon was there. I can't really remember anything else."

I am surprised that I received no grief from being on the basketball court, but maybe they thought I hooped at school. Thank God Marlon is a solid ass brother.

I recover incredibly fast for someone who thought that he was dying, & quickly realize that Rico withheld some details from me. He did not merely find a gun.

The whole fucking thing is confusing! The "discarded" gun is a murder weapon... to someone in the neighborhood which is way too close of a coincidence.

"Why would someone toss a murder weapon so close to where the homicide was?" I think to myself, but in order to get the necessary answers, I need to approach the source.

I hobble around the block to where Rico lives. I have not been going to school because, well you know I was shot. The bullet went through my chest & landed in a beam in the wall where It became evidence.

I will not give Rico a chance to come up with another lie. I decide not to disclose what we learned from detective Latham.

Knock Knock

I knock on Rico's door. Homes in the hood lack doorbells.

"Hey Robby, how have you been, baby boy?"

Dangerous Dachel. Sigh, if I could have avoided her, I would have. Dachel is Rico's cousin, or some close relative...it never really mattered to me. She gives me a genuine embracing hug.
We have history. She's a petite woman with thick hips, & almond eyes. Her lips are pure pink, & I'm talking about both sets. She is the hood's unicorn. Everyone wants to mount her.

It is unfathomable that she gave me a chance. Out of all the people in the hood, why me? I believe my self-esteem is showing.

"I'm good love. What's new with you?" I reply.

"Not a thing, just cooling it. Sorry bout what happened. See this is why you should have run away with......never mind." She teases & snickers as she shakes her head reminiscing about the times we had.

Oh, to remember the times. I am sure she is referencing when we experimented with the coconut massage oil. Just imagining licking the cream off of her glistening brown cheeks. The tender areas of her body revealed by the candlelight. That image stays with me even when I shut my eyes....it gives me satisfaction.

I almost forgot that I am on a mission.

"You say that every time I see you yo," I reply, fake outraged. She is a tease incarnate. The very thing that reels you in just a little bit & when you are finally close, you can feel the blue balls.

"Well if you must know, Whoo & I don't talk anymore." She slyly retorts.

"What a shocker!" Says Rico descending the steps clumsily wearing soggy mismatch socks which is unlike him. his entire outfit is perturbing. Rico wouldn't ever let the hood see him in that struggle fit. He rapidly stuffs his cellphone in his pocket.

Hmm, suspicion #1. Something is off.

"I gotta talk to you bruh." Dachel instinctively exits.

"Bye Robby, we shall finish our debate." Dachel teases.

"Get a fucking room damn." Rico quips.

"I'll catch up with you some other time love," I conclude.

Dachel is the bridge that connects Rico & I. I knew her & pursued her before Rico ever moved in with her. Then one random summer, he came through & it's been history ever since. He stuck with me even after she & I fell off, but boy if I could change the dynamics of our relationship, I would.

I observe her every step & retrace every curve on her body.

"Man, I'm sorry for what happened to you, you are like a brother to me, you know I would never blast you fam!"

"It's aight. I'm not saying we even nigga, just know it didn't end my life, a real nigga leaves on his own feet you feel me? Plus, it makes me more gangsta when I tell everybody I was shot. Bitches love thugs. "I joke awkwardly. "But for real, I gotta tell you something. That gun matches the one used to kill that man up the street from my spot. What you know about that?"

"....Yea I know. I wasn't even supposed to have that shit. Whoo gave it to me to hide in the spot...I was with him the night he murked Mr. Stevens! I stood right there, I encouraged him to do it." Rico confesses.

There's the Rico I love & hate. Always attempting to fit in to be someone he is not. He is just slightly cool that no one in the hood looks at him sideways. I understand him & hate him for the fact that his goal in the hood is to belong. One cannot play both sides of the fence, yet Rico does it with precision. He will chill with the niggas that dog us, & then watch some anime with Marlon & I seconds afterward. I know he does not participate in the slander, but it didn't help relations between us & the neighborhood. It's always "The Peters V. Everyone".

Rico is one of the people who are first in line to defend me when he first relocated here. He says that when he is around the others in the neighborhood, they do not talk about us much, which is debatable. I usually take his word for it. He is cool off of the strength of him being black & Puerto Rican, with earrings & dressing similar to rappers. When I first saw him at Dachel's, I thought he was a pretty boy that would not associate with someone like me, but we gravitated towards one another genuinely despite me piping down his kin.

"So, this entire time you knew Whoo murked him, I'm not telling you to snitch but, you could have at least let me know what it was. You told him to murk him? Why?"

I am furious because I already despise Whoo for his involvement in the deterioration of my relationship with Dachel. Not to mention how bad he makes the neighborhood with his toxicity & drugs. His name gives me a bitter taste. I would hawk spit after each annunciation of the letters in his street name.

Whoo is a local drug dealer. To make things worse, Dachel relinquished her vagina to him even though he did nothing for her. Even though he can never love her the way I have. Even though I provided nothing to Dachel, those refund checks sure had a nigga feeling like a million bucks, even if they were $500.

"You brought the heat down on him dug, eventually he's going to find out what happened."

"He already knows man!" Rico replies while simultaneously shaking his head. "But I will figure something out."

"True, true." I guess he wants me to shrug it off. I was not about to allow him to half-ass me, besides my guard is way up.

Suspicion #2. Hmm, why is he being so nonchalant? I hate that shit.

"But Um. Aye, walk me around the block real quick I gotta swing through my man's crib." Rico invites.
"What mans?" I ask curiously.

"You don't know him, just bop with me real quick unless ya chest fucking with you, I know them old ass lungs ain't what they used to be, how I been dunking on you." Rico evades.

I know I am not popular, but I been around long enough. Niggas ain't just moving in that I don't know of. East Baltimore is compact, plus, I don't drive so my means of transportation are my feet. I know everyone, especially the people that don't like me. I always keep intel on the antagonists. My "Spidey senses" are jumping the fuck off. Hmm...

Suspicion #3. What niggas do you know that I don't know?

Trenches

Shake Sumthin

It is a bit strange to me, I know pretty much everyone Rico does, & this is the first time I hear about a "homie" around the corner. I give him the benefit of the doubt though seeing as we are not always joined at the hip. Nonetheless, I proceed to walk with him.

I watch the sunset & ponder Rico's predicament. Perhaps he is just buying some weed....him & his weak ass "reggie".

We arrive at where Rico's "imaginary friend" resides & I wait on the stoop for Rico to handle his business so we can dip. My wound is aching now which is Rico jinxing me by talking about my lungs.

"It's cool you can come in, he's good peep." Rico persuades.

I step up the first 3 marble steps & make my way to the basement where Rico plus an obvious addict leads me to.

"A crack head sells reggie huh?" I snicker to myself. Reggie is the slang term for bullshit weed in the hood.

As I step down the basement steps into this unrestricted space, there are 3 guys waiting which includes Whoo.

"What's up Rico?" Shouts Whoo as he ignores my presence.

"Not much what's up?" Rico responds.

"Well I hear we have a conundrum, but it's nothing that can't be ironed out."

"Man I brought Robert as you requested, it's no reason for me to be down here, I don't want to be a witness to this. Imma dip!" Rico protests as he points his thumb in the direction of the stairs from which we came. Those are the stairway to heaven for Rico, he led me down to hell & wants to just skate on with the rest of his life as if I shot him. Petty!

Rico has the nerve to plot like this against me when he's the one in the wrong. He's talking like he brought me as if I didn't confront him at his house. Basically he was coming to meet me & lead me to this place. No wonder he was so off. The guilt is basically seeping from his pores.

"Nigga this a setup?!! So you brought me here to get Whoo & them to intimidate me because you wanted to play with his ratchet??" I let loose. "Oh nah we not going down like that. I told you a real nigga go out on his own, guess we know you not a real nigga. I should have known cause you fuck with them niggas around the way & play the fifty."

"Oh so that's what happened? Ha, everything that's done in the dark shall come to the light." Whoo preaches. "So what do you think I should do? Technically yo ain't do shit wrong. You the one playing with the burner that I told you to stash for me. You shouldn't even have had it on you. Ain't no nigga trying out you in the hood. You outed yourself, lor nigga"

"Listen I just wanted to be down with the yea...You told me to bring Robby, now he's here. Are we gucci?" Rico pleads.

"Boy you a fluke, Imma tell you what," Whoo proceeds to taunt while he draws his gun. The same heavy piece of metal that chastised me. I'm about to get a second dose of that scorpion sting, & I'm not even out of pain from the first! Fuck! Same gun, but this time it is extended. He added a silencer on the barrel. Just what a scorpion needs, an even bigger stinger.

I imagine the same yellow tape will be here as the one that is still currently blowing in the wind on the side of my house. I can see the newspaper article now, "Local Teen Caught up in Drugs Murdered in the Basement of a Crack House." "Don't forget to attach a picture of me from my high school yearbook", I thought.

I am about to die in this dingy ass basement corridor. Bullshit! I scope & observe everything I can. The walls are pale blue, but it is not as apparent with the dim ass light bulb swinging profusely. The walls appear pee-stained from the light. Too many bricks are exposed, this house is probably uninhabitable.

There is a blanket on the floor under our feet, plus there is a kitty litter odor that emanates all around us, yet I did not catch a glimpse of any cats when we arrived.

"Man I'll do whatever you want just don't kill me Whoo please. I turned my head when you were fucking with Dachel!"

"Nigga you act like I needed your permission...your blessing. Fuck outta here!"
Whoo ignores Rico's cries & acknowledges me.

"This nigga is willing to rat you out to clean his conscience as long as another nigga falls for him. How does that make you feel? He's willing to crucify you."
"You know I'm a religious man. You a damn Judas, Rico! And for that...Robert you are going to have to burn him." Whoo directs.

I'm shocked. Rico is Whoo's A1. They are practically family, but Whoo's making me burn him?!
"Nah man I'm not going go out like that. He's a bitch, a pussy, & a fluke, but I'm not about that life. You don't have to kill him nor me. You can let us both walk & I still will keep my mouth shut about the whole situation for real." I reply, gaining all composure.

"Robby. If you don't smoke him, Imma have to smoke you & then Imma smoke your brother. He leaves out for school at 8:09 am. It's not personal it's the way shit is." Whoo insists. "Too many loose ends & too many witnesses courtesy of ya boy Rico here."

"Whoo it was a fucking mistake. Don't kill me please I'll kill him give me the piece." Rico pleads.

I know what's clear & that I implemented Marlon into this bs.

Something in me changed.

I took the piece & hesitate. I hesitate, I hesitate...**Blickup!** I shoot Rico in the arm.

"Robby I'm sorry?!!" Rico cries as spit runs down his Hollister shirt.

"Don't drag it out, don't make shorty suffer." Whoo continues.

I would kill for Marlon & Rico, but now I am killing Rico for Marlon.

Blickup! Blickup! Blickup!

I empty 3 slugs into Rico's head & watch his eyes roll back.

When his body hit the floor, the force of his skull ricocheting sounds like dice on concrete.
He is gone. His face grew pale & his eyes become cloudy. Life has vacated this young man.

Hands still shaking, & tears in my eyes. Blood is thicker than water I convince myself.......

Something in me changed that day.

Trenches

Unfortunate Circumstances

"Ashes to ashes, & dust to dust. I commit this young man's body to the ground from which it came."

Reverend Carter presides over Rico's funeral. I attend of course, hey I still possess some morals. Besides, it will appear highly suspicious that his best friend, was a no show. Standing at this cemetery I watch his casket descend into the ground, I could not help but reflect back to when I was questioned by Detective Latham.

"Robert Peters. Do you go by any street names or nicknames?"

"My family & friends call me Robby....& females," I reply.

He chuckles. "A ladies man huh? Well try if you can to remember what you can about the incident. Did you smell anything out of sorts? Like a distinct smell? Perfume? Cologne? Did you see anyone? Robert do you know the shooter?"

He tries to throw me off my game with the last question. "No to all of it detective. I know what you know man. It happened too quickly for me to surmise or speculate on who the perpetrator or perpetrators were." I surprise him with my vocabulary. It is nothing special, I spend much of my time watching CSI: Miami with my mom, so the lingo is fluid.

I drift back into the present moment. I meet many different members of Rico's immediate & distant family. Some faces are familiar & welcoming. Others are uninviting as I cannot stand to look at them knowing that I am the catalyst for each & every emotion they are feeling. There are faces that are full of sorrow, hatred & unrest.

The groundskeeper continues to crank the handle, and Rico continues to be lowered into an abyss.

It is a nice casket, black adorned with gold trims. There is even a gold plaque with his name on it on the outside head of the casket.

The local March Funeral Home took care of the entire process. I stand next to Dachel as she sobs & clings to me.

I know if I told her what happened that I will never get her back. At least not the way I want her back. I observe the black eyeliner begin to creep & ponder, "Do I even want her back?" The fact that I am focused on her attractiveness in her time of need re-challenges my morality & remorse. At a time like this I am observing the makeup on her face instead of the makeup used to cover the bullet hole in my deceased friends' skull. I need to prioritize which feelings in my psyche to attack first.

I recite a comforting mantra, " to be absent from the body is to be present with the lord. Rico knew better."

"What? Robby, what was Rico into?" She asks.

My abrupt & out loud thinking has alarmed Dachel. I shush her to distract her from pursuing an answer to her question.

"What's up Robert how you hanging? You good, you straight?" Tevin asks.
Tevin is Rico's cousin. I consider him a mutual friend. Although he & Rico had a falling out over a game system, Tevin remained "cool".

"I'm gucci," I reply. I am careful not to reveal my inner turmoil.

"Yeah it's fucking ridiculous. Of all people, who would have foreseen that Rico would end up gunned down by some crack head while trying to buy weed?" Tevin asserts.

Pause for a minute!

The newspaper "The Baltimore Sun" releases a story detailing Rico's death by this "reggie" selling hippy crack head. They continue to even connect the crack head to my shooting & the shooting of Mr. Stevens.

They pin three bodies on him Because Whoo intimidated him to take the fall. It was either jail or death, with the latter being too great of a disposition.

Not to mention the police found Rico's body slumped behind a dumpster in the back of Smitty's liquor store. The evidence is scattered, which Whoo made sure of. No one can trace it back to him because he took all measures to negate accountability for the shooting. Besides he is not the shooter, I am.

I drift back to earlier when everyone is present at church for the wake. I walk up to the casket with my mother. She says, "It's amazing what a little makeup can do to a body that has been broken."

My heart sinks. Though my mother never suspected me of involvement in the murder, if she ever asks, I cannot be anything but truthful. I cannot lie to moms... not again anyway.

"Yea he looks at peace." I begin choking & tears flood my eyesight. "I don't know how Imma get through this ma. I don't know how to stop feeling." I exhale. The air erupts from deep in my bones which causes more pain in my wound.

"You have family, & God to help you with that Robby."

God is a joke, if he never put me in this predicament, I would be living normally with my best friend by my side. But blaming God gives me no peace nor satisfaction. I know that I can never ask God to heal my heart for what I did. I should blame Satan.

I am justified in killing a traitor, but it still does not assist my conscience at night. I compromised my morals. I have a bone to pick with myself.

.........Remember son, "to be absent from your body is to be present with the Lord."

Trenches

Opening Up Shop

In the past few weeks I notice an improvement in my outlook at life. At one point I considered suicide just to be even with Rico, but I convince myself that he is somewhere that I cannot afford to visit.

......Which is partially true.

"Good game fellas," I say as I wipe the sweat from my face. There are a few dudes who actually grew to respect Marlon & I. With age brought maturity I guess, or maybe they pitied me because

I lost the only person who fucked with me.

I walk to Miss Peggy's corner store & purchase a beverage. I do not care what the flavor is, as long as the physical color is blue. As I exit Miss Peggy's, I immediately bump into Whoo's partner Kirk, the same guy who was in the basement with Rico, Whoo & I. I did not know his government until I started asking around about him. In my eyes they are still my enemies & I needed as much more Intel on them as possible.

"Watch it shordy!" Kirk hollers.

"Nah you watch it dug!" I defend. I am not that same scared black boy any longer because I no longer fear death. Death was present in the pissy room with me when I pulled the trigger. Death stood idle by the day I was awarded a hole in my chest.

Now what I really fear most is death taking my brother who is away pursuing something that has been unattainable in my family. Marlon has started a process that can reverse the cycle of men in our family for the next generations. He escaped this trend and for that I fear for his life.

"Ha-ha you think you got nuts.

"Man whatever." I wave my hand dismissing him then cut through the alley to get back home.
Whoo chases me down on my way back.

"I didn't tell the cops nothing" I blurt while surrendering my hands up in the air spilling juice on my hooping shoes. I loved these shoes they are white with grey Nike Air Too Strong.

"Chill out, it's not even like that. I have a great deal of respect for you protecting your family. Plus you held shit down as a real nigga should. That's why I have a proposition that you might be interested in. I'm sure you know my operation, come to the spot to holler at me trigger boy. "

I continue home contemplating what it is to be in the middle or upper class in Maryland. Would I even be in contact with these types of individuals if my parents graduated from college? I head upstairs to grab my blade off of my rickety dresser adventuring to Whoo's place on Asquith Street.

It is a tall 3 story brick building that junkies frequent often. Consistent rain has contributed to the natural wear & tear of the building causing the bricks to appear faded.

I always get off the bus in front of the "Empire of Doom" as Marlon & I nickname it. We will walk pass Miss Peggy's store up the street to our house. Many times we bought snacks from the store before we went home, scavenging up whatever change we can find.

I scan the building & notice a few of Whoo's gang outside of the front entrance incognito. They are sitting in lawn chairs wearing black tees. I start to profile them. Both men are tatted up & appear to care for nothing. These are the type of guys you put on the front line of the battlefield to slow down the opposing battalion.

Kirk who I had beef with prior shows me around. He is the epitome of a "hood nigga" tour guide. The journey is not long physically, but mentally it is an adventure.

"And this room here....nigga you listening? This room here is where we keep the percs. We cut them in 2's with a razor selling them for double what they go for down the hill." Kirk says.

"Whoo wants you to be his lookout kid. As you know that was one of the things Rico did poorly, God rest his dead soul." Kirk is being facetious & it shows all over his black face with his black grin.

The way Kirk describes the situation intrigues me. I could make some money plus I won't have to touch any product. At this point, I already dropped all of my classes at the University of Baltimore in order to not get an F. My job will be to alert the dope boys of any unknowns passing by.

Unknowns are cars that are unfamiliar within our area. Cars that may swing through the block multiple times without any clear destination. They are the most dangerous & detrimental to drug dealers because the knockers can use any car they wish & hop out on them.

"Over here is the cocoa room, we cook all of the Crack in here. You don't need to know any of this information but Whoo insists you know what we move. We have a lot of junkies who try getting in here so you may have to be on the lookout for that too."

The room is filthy, it's a beige-colored room with a makeshift stove. They cook the coke on a canister burner, which looks like a science class lab room. Salt is everywhere & the spoons are covered in dried up cocaine residue plus baking powder.

There are boxes of baking soda & sugar empty on the floor in the corner. The smell of ammonia is destroying my brain cells. It is interesting though; I have never been up close to a drug operation. The most I have ever seen is capsules on the playground. I contribute my curiosity to my watching of CSI: Miami because I am clueless about the other side of the law.

"How come you guys have not gotten kicked in?" I ask.

"Easy nigga, let's just say this room ain't here, it's invisible so keep that in mind. We fan and air out the room through special vents to keep the ammonia & bleach smells out. You damn near have to wear a mask to stay alive otherwise."

"But you don't have to worry about that" replies Whoo smiling profusely. "You are the neighborhood lookout; no product will be trusted to you. We keep going this business going by not having so many hands in the pot you feel me?"

"Your house is on the corner, the best place to see any unknowns coming down Aiken Street. Plus I need you to hold excess money that any dealer brings to you."

"But won't that bring attention if the knockers happen to see dudes running back & forth from the block to my yard?" I ask.

"Smart. I've had East North Avenue on lock for a minute, you think I haven't worked the ins & outs of slinging? There are more lookouts than just you. No knockers should be able to see anything if you report correctly. You Rob, just focus on the task which is to get paid. There will be a schedule of who & when they will be dropping off. I do not have to reiterate the seriousness or responsibility of my money. That is more important than ya life understand that. This is business."

This is not a bad deal actually. I will get eighty dollars each day that I am on the lookout which I can use since I no longer receive refund checks from college. Lately my lack of motivation has driven my obsession with cause & effect duality themes. The death of Rico only magnifies my discourse. Hanging & hooping in the neighborhood has me feeling more secluded. What else can I do except......

Get Money!!!!!

"So when do I start?"

I am young, broke & stupid. This is a severe lapse of judgment. It is the kind of decision that unnecessary of an angel or devil posted up on either shoulder telling me the pros & cons because even the devil will convince me that this is fucked up.

....Even Lucifer is smart enough not to get in bed with another devil.

Trenches

A Lick!

I have been a lookout for about a year now, & I am complaint-free. No laws are being broken that I consider important anyways.

"Ay yoooooo! 5 0 hitting the block shordy. Does anybody hear me? Uniformed officers."

I hate using these walkie-talkies because they come in scratchy as shit. Besides Kirk bought them from Walgreen's up the street. Cheap equipment for an empire. If I run a business "I will never cut corners" I think to myself.

"Aight Rob, good alert. I got some extra money I need to drop off. Be outback in 20."

"Aight." I make sure not to use Paul's name on the radio. Paul is on the ground selling rock. He watches the streets after I point out the unknowns & cops. He uses the basketball game as a cover after the cops disperse.

20 minutes later

I run out back & open the door anticipating Paul's arrival.

"Hey Robby." Angie greets. "You have a friend here waiting for you. Uh, Paul is his name I believe. Don't be out here long baby."

"Yes ma'am," I reply.

I make sure to wear cargo pants or shorts when I accept extra money so that my pockets look unsuspecting. I say my "what's up" to Paul then quickly take the dough as he peels off.
After I close the back door & walk into the dining room. My mother Angie sidesteps in front of me lecturing on the premises of.......

"I don't want you hanging around that boy Robby. I know what he does & what everyone around here does for that matter. I'm not about to let you fall in front of nobody's bad deeds. I had my suspicions about Rico, but I let it slide. Now I'm saying something out of love."

"But ma he not even like that he wanted to hold the basketball that's it." Moms are always suspicious, but I shrug her off. Sooner or later she will find out what's going on unless I quit. She pretty much has it all summed up & her suspicions are definitely warranted. A mother's intuition. A mom knows when she knows.

Today feels weird. I feel like something bad is going to take place because I had a dream envisioning my grandmother last night. I woke up in a cold sweat trying to convince myself that I had not dreamt her up. "No, no, no shit!" I scream as I wake up & chuck my pillows in the corner of the room. I threw them in the direction she stood as she glares at me with such contempt.

Each dream is the same. She never says anything or moves. She just stares, piercing me with her eyes, the same ones that my mom use to peer through me. It is the most haunting thing I have ever encountered & though she cannot harm me physically, her image is enough to psychologically scar me up until my late adulthood. "Who you gonna call?"

Grandma is always a bad omen in our family. She is a premonition for bad events to come. Whenever my mom or I see her something bad happens like death or losing money. The list goes on about the possible things she could be forewarning us of.

I snap myself out of thinking about that eerie dream, hallucination, or vision, whatever it was. The screeches from the static force me back to the present.

"Yo this John I got some dough with me come pick up I need to drop off before 12 comes."
"Aight I'm on my way," I respond not sure why John is bringing extra dough because Whoo has it worked out that only Paul will be necessary to drop off excess profit to not arouse more suspicions from the boys in blue. I shrug it off & take the cash I just received from Paul & stash it in the dresser. I take the drawer out & put the cash in the bottom where there is empty space.

That is the best hiding place I can think of aside from the ceiling. Now all I need is a rottweiler or pit to protect the house.

I go out back after I find my mother lying down in her room relaxing from work.
Once I open the door...

WHOP!!!

I'm caught off guard & hit in the face with the butt of a gun. Some nigga has John hemmed up by his collar demanding money.

"Where the cash at dummy?"
"I don't have any dug; he's the first drop tell him!!"

"Just give him the money Rob come on it ain't even worth dying over." John pleads as he wipes his bloody nose.

It never occurs to John that he just ratted me out that I have cash with me. Damn John! Shit that's not my money I can't get that back.

WINNING THE LOTTO WOULD BE NICE!

My ear still rings from that sneak attack. I hope I don't lose my hearing. Is that what Is most important? My hearing? I am worried about my hearing!

Number 1 a nigga has a gun to my head.

Number 2 a nigga will have a gun to my head when I tell him I lost his money.

Number 3 my mom's is in the other room knocked out...for now.

Yea it is safe to say I am fine with losing hearing in both my ears, along with my sense of taste & smell.

Shit, it is better than going to Whoo empty-handed I figure. I go upstairs with this nigga holding the gun at the back of my neck. I won't attempt to make any sudden moves; shit I was shot once before. I am not trying to be in that predicament again....& especially not if it endangers moms.
I reach under the bed to grab my cut of the money that I remember I keep separate from Whoo's.

"Here nigga this is it all," I shout still clutching my sore ear. He begins to back up as if he's on the firing squad. He does not even count it he just backs up then suddenly makes a break down the steps with John following him.

Shit, I never figured John went to art school because that nigga definitely majored in acting. Definitely never pegged him for the betraying type.

I get on the walkie-talkie, "yo, yo somebody hit Whoo up. Tell him I got ambushed."

"Ambush?"

"Yea ambush, John & some nigga robbed me of the bread!"
Shit I have to get that dough back man. One way or another. I neglect to tell them John only got my cut because it is smaller & I see an opportunity to come up.
"...but tell Whoo Imma make it back yo."

I do not know how or where, but this was nothing to take lightly. I cannot risk my life or my loved ones, this is non-negotiable.

I am waist-deep in a nightmare.

"Rico, Grandma.... watch over me!"

I am young, broke & stupid. This is a severe lapse of judgment. It is the kind of decision that unnecessary of an angel or devil posted up on either shoulder telling me the pros & cons because even the devil will convince me that this is fucked up.

....Even Lucifer is smart enough not to get in bed with another devil.

Trenches

Rather You than Me

Whoo is on me to make this money back. He warned me, & though I took his words seriously, it's nothing that I could have done to prevent from being robbed. I am being greedy though. I gave up my cut of the money I made & kept Whoo's which only exacerbates my conscience.

I imagine the angel & devil poof onto each shoulder to criticize me for trying to come up. But nonetheless I found a solution to my dilemma.

I wait until sunset to dip out to complete my mission. I am informed of a potential stickup that can bag me way more than what I already owe Whoo. If this fails, I will have to just swap out the money that is originally Whoo's & pocket what I make from the robbery.

"Down Da Hill" is South of where I live, but is still East Baltimore, just "cruddier" around there.

I buy a 38 revolver from Paul's connect. I don't really know how to use it, but I am informed it does not discharge shells which means less evidence, but only get 6 shots.

I heard rumors from Paul that a nigga named Rell just got a lick off some white boys from the county. Rell supposedly killed his cousin in order to keep all of the money for himself. But we all know how rumors in the hood go. I hear he is "grimy" but sheesh to kill your own blood for bread. I guess it's not out of the ordinary considering my best friend set me up.

Rell is in his late 20s, a known killer. He is the man in Baltimore. Every description of him includes the word ruthless, & savage. He never gives a fuck who he crosses. Shit he would probably cross his own mother.

He stays on Monument Street & Broadway. I walk down with a baggy sweatshirt on plus my Nike air too Strong's for a quick in & out. I have the gun tucked in my pants in the back with a rolled-up face mask on top of my head which is typical Baltimore attire in the hood.

If I do not get this money, Whoo will kill me, or worst my family. "I gotta stop implementing my family in this shit" I berate myself.

After half an hour of walking, I finally make it to his neck of the woods. The walk isn't far nor long at all, but my fear has me taking small and short steps. Along the way I turned around twice to go home but I considered that this mission is mandatory if I'm to harden my soul. My greed got the best of me.

It is dark as hell & there is no one outside of where Paul claims Rell is always posted up at.
"Fuck! I hope I'm not going have to run up in his spot. I am by myself so that is a stupid move, but I cannot wait him out all night." I ponder.

"Nigga who would you take Jordan, LeBron, Kobe, or A.I. ?"

"Shit Jordan all day you heard me?!"

"Shit I bet Rell going say bum ass LeBron."

I overhear dudes talk from around the corner. It's my lucky day because one of them niggas says Rell's name plus he fits the description.

They are posted up on the back steps drinking, smoking & debating the best ballplayer. "I could run up bust-a-move, get em all by surprise. Or I could pick them off one by one. But I'm not trying to kill nobody though," I thought. Besides the numbers are against me.

I wait until I feel like "fuck it gotta get this shit over with." I move slowly with my back against the wall of the brick houses. I slowly draw my gun from my back. I have it aimed at the ground.

In 2 feet I will be out of cover. Shit, I realize I play too many shooter games, what a nerd.

"Yo I'm about to take a piss, hold my drink & don't burn the whole blunt." Rell is lit which is perfect for me. I wait until he's inside the adjacent vacant alley to make my move.

Pssssssssssss... The sound of Rell urinating.

"Don't move dug," I say with a low voice. You got that bread? Where it's at?"

"What bread nigga?!" Rell replies.

I hear the coldness in his voice. He's a killer, not an accident killer. He is dark skin, teeth are rotted yellow, actually, those are his gold fronts. He has on a Louis Vuitton belt & dopes. This man's energy is intimidating to say the least. I don't feel fear from him, as if he wakes up and accepts his fate every day.

I hit him with the gun, "bitch run your pockets!" He turns around to look at me simultaneously removing everything from his pockets. I forgot I never rolled the face mask down! Fuck! But it's dark so maybe he will not remember my face.

He has a grip of about 5 grand, a green dot card, a set of Acura car keys plus an iPhone 5. Shit that was more than enough to cover what I owe.

"I want it all," whispers the devil on my shoulder.

"Thought you ain't have nothing fuck boy." I tease. "Right, right, right."

"You must be from up North, you gotta be from Harford Road huh?" He asks.

"Yea none of that matters pimp," I reply.

"You got that North Avenue ass, wannabe ass, voice nigga. Fake ass hood nigga. You must not know what I do, but when I catch you Imma put a bullet in ya brain. Straight up." Rell confidently replies.

"Yea aight." As soon as I pocket all of his former property, I notice voices coming around the corner.

"Ay yo over here, I'm getting jacked! Get the tone!" Rell warns.

I spent too much time alerting his friends to the lack of his presence. The sound of the tennis shoes against the turf startles me & I accidentally pull the trigger.

Boooooooowwwwwwww!

"Shit nigga shot me in the ass!"

I shoot Rell in his butt & skedaddle! I didn't mean to, but I didn't care either.
Shit they stop running towards me anyways which gave me time to getaway. It's not like he can get in his car & chase me down. No one shot back so I assume they weren't packing.

I make my way home eventually; the walk takes half as long since I know my way back. I sneak back in the house through the unlocked back door & creep upstairs. I collapse on my bed with the gun still in my hand.

I didn't change, didn't put anything away...I just sleep.

This shit is going to kill me one way or another. The pound of my heart beating drowns me & gives way to a massive anxiety headache. I grab the trash can by my bed and vomit in it uncontrollably. I weigh my demons & count sheep which helps me drift off easier than I ever have any other night. This hot sweat put me out.

Trenches

Brother's Keeper

I wake up to the sun searing my brown eyes. Someone has opened the blinds in my room, but have they seen anything? I look at my hand which is no longer clutching the gun. I am a bit disoriented & confused.

Am I still dreaming? Maybe the last few years of my life were a dream & I am ready to come back from it all. One thing for sure, my headache has disappeared, & I am ready to "seize the day" which I recollected from some informational commercial's slogan.

Every intricate detail is hazy which leads me to believe that I was possibly in a coma, & my mind is imagining histories & futures that I never lived through. Hood fantasies perhaps.
...How unlikely.

"The fuck?!" I hop up fast, my heart jumps twice as fast when I see Marlon sitting on my dresser. He stares at me in disbelief & fear. The kid he grew up with has morphed into a sinister menace.
His facial expressions & demeanor are warranted though. I am far from the church-going moral young man that my mother brags about. I have not been to church in forever, & school is an extracurricular activity I have no need for at the moment.

"Nigga you scared the shit outta me! What's up when you come back?" I greet.

Marlon's participating in an internship for the University of Baltimore in New York. He has been away for about 6 months ever since the situation around Lafayette deteriorated further. It seems to be an escape from these trenches. He has been up to date with some of the things that have happened back home but mainly busy focusing on success.

"What the fuck is up with you yo?" Marlon asks.

"Hold on let me lock the door," I whisper. "Where's the gun? Where's the money?"

"Everything is in your bins."

I have 2 bins, a green & a blue one which I keep miscellaneous items in. My high-school diploma is in one of them along with my prom pictures, some comic books & some of my dad's old Playboy magazines that he horribly hid.

I start to lash out, "Marlon you been away for a while, shit has changed. Shit has changed for me in ways you wouldn't respect if I told you."

"Nigga all you had to do is c....."

"You weren't here for me! When Rico died, nah you weren't there for me when I had to go to the funeral with only mom there. You didn't pick up a phone, you ain't hit my shit!" I interrupt.
"I had a chance to do something, so I took it!" Marlon replies.

"You know if it wasn't for me, you would be dead! Fuck your internship if I didn't kill Rico, Whoo was going to pop you!" I blurt.

I didn't mean to fumble those words out, especially like that, but shit it happened.
"What! You ain't kill him, what are you talking about?" Marlon asks perplexed.

I run him through the story making sure to spare no details so he will put himself in my shoes & feel awful about abandoning me.

"D...damn Robby. Shit is unbelievable. My fault, I should have been checking up on the family. It seems I always wanted to get away from here, but I forgot I left the most important people in 1300."

I relinquish my sins from my chest which finally allows me to think logically. I had no one to talk to in forever.
"So Whoo is the root of all this shit?" Marlon asks.

"Yea for the most part but don't worry about him, his time coming. Walk me to the store though, I need something to drink. They don't keep no juice in this damn house."

It's just like old times again. We never travel anywhere without one another; we are attached at the hip. "Oh wait a min, let me check the block and let the fellas know I'm coming out."
"Yo I'm hitting Miss Peggy's real quick.".... No response. "Let me peer outside" I think to myself.

I peek through my blinds & see a black Acura driving down the street. The windows roll down & I see Rell's "cruddy" face.

He is very resourceful, what tipped him off?

Trenches

Flashbacks

I have been staying low key during these last few weeks. It is only a matter of time before Rell catches me lacking.

Rell & his guys keep appearing around Aiken street during the last 3 weeks. Luckily for me, I am a lookout boy in the sky. I see everything so I know when he comes through. But if I was on the ground with everyone else, I would probably have a couple more holes in my head.

I find out through Paul that Whoo knows Rell from a prior stint in central booking. Some messed up drug charges, but both served about a year.

"Fuck it I'm coming out today" I thought. Marlon is still asleep from us hitting my homie Lawrence's kickback.

I get up to walk down the steps. Each step creaks louder than the last.

Eek! Eek, eek!

Fuck it I just run down the rest of them. "Robby, morning!"

Damn I woke his ass up. "What's he going to complain & lecture me about this time?" I thought. The last thing I need to hear this dreary morning is how much of a failure I am.

"Hey dad. Good morning."

"Since you're going downstairs, grab me a glass of cold water would you & make sure the kitchen windows are down it is supposed to rain."

"Yes sir!"

"Shit if it rains, I'm off for the day" I thought. The walkie-talkies get scrambled by the rain for some reason. Yea cheap equipment I think to myself again.

"Man Its cuddling weather. Imma hit up Dachel today since I'm not doing anything" I say to myself. I walk in the kitchen, shut each window then proceed to get my father some ice water.
I walk back to my parent's room & give my dad his water.

"Thanks son. Oh uh we need to talk later on."

I figure he is going to tell me he understands why I dropped out or took the semester off, whatever I want to define it as. Basically, it is time to get off my ass & start contributing to the household is what I surmise will be the summary of this "pleasant" chat.

"Ok I'll be back in a few so we can chat later on pops," I reply.
 We never really have much to say to one another.
 I pick up the phone & dial.

4 1 0 7 2 7 8 2 8 8

ring

"Hello."

"Hey what's up Dachel love?"

"Hey boy what's up?" Dachel replies.

"Not much what you doing? You miss me?"

"Just a little bit" she teases. "Why, are you coming over?" She asks.

"Yea I'll be there in 5. Imma shower at your place lady."

"Aight." She hangs up the phone.
I leave in a dark blue hoodie that covers the majority of my face. If Rell comes out here, he will not be able to identify me easily. I tuck my gun just in case.

I make my way to Dachel's & knock. It takes her about 40 seconds to come down the steps wrapped in a towel.

"Damn that's how are you feeling??!" I exclaim.

"Yea that's exactly how I'm feeling. How long has it been since you hit this? Do you still remember what I taste like?" She teases.

"Too long, way too long. I was partying yesterday but got in at 4:00 am so I ain't get a chance to wash or nothing Imma be like 10 mins don't start without me."

"Ok Robby" she replies with a devious smile.

I ascend the stairs & head into the bathroom so casually because, well I am still familiar to her place. I can feel the entire aura of our encounters. I have those butterflies as if it's the first time again, but they will subside As they always do. I will admit throughout this turmoil, my confidence has skyrocketed.

I hop in the shower which feels awesome. I just let the warm water bead off my skin & gravity pulls them down into the drain. Man I missed showering. On Lafayette, we only have a tub that lacked a showerhead & rod, so we make do with taking baths. I start wiping the water from my face when Dachel enters.

"I thought you already jumped in?" I say.

"I did but I can't wait for you any longer!"

She takes me by my penis & pulls me closer for a kiss. I shut the water off & lead her into her own room.

For a moment I mentally pause because on the way, we pass Rico's old room. I envision him sitting in his bean bag chair smoking a blunt. It is hella eerie.

It's so surreal, but like the smoke he puffs, his image went up & dissipates. I throw her on the bed & lick her from her shoulder blades to each butt cheek as she lays on her stomach. I turn her over & kiss her from each breast to the defined V-shape pelvic area. Her butt is so plump & full that it rises off the bed making her back slant over it. She is excellent at yoga.

"You know how much I miss you Robby?" She asks.

"Shut up! Show me!" I begin gripping her throat & stroke as I feel her get creamier.
I care less about a condom, & even less about pulling out. It does not take me long to bust as I came in maybe 4 minutes, but that's to be expected.

It's basically new pussy to me because I had not hit it in God knows how long.
Since she did not climax, I eat her pussy until she squirts. I then clean myself up, unimpressed by my performance.

"Damn Robby, are we making this an ongoing thing?" Dachel asks.

"Maybe. Who knows how you will feel in a few weeks."?

I know I am clinging due to desperation. I have not talked to anyone except Marlon. I had a little situation before all of this madness in Lafayette though. Well, I wouldn't necessarily call it a situation as much as me holding onto someone that I was pressed over. I used to date this girl from the University of Baltimore named Tamika. I forced her to take up the title of "girlfriend". She was not ready for that when I proposed the idea to her.

I broke up with Tamika when I caught her talking to my sister Erica's homeboy. Plus I found out she was nothing but a confused bird who didn't know if she liked men or women. Me making her choose to settle down was eye-opening though. From then on, I vowed to never force anything.
Not love, not relationships & definitely not acceptance.

I start to reassemble my belongings & my clothing but Dachel just lies there naked eyeing me. She turns on her side which is my invitation to cuddle her, the very purpose of my journey.
I take off the little clothes that I managed to rapidly put back on & leave my gun under my hoodie sitting on the floor under her charcoal black desk. This desk has seen some of the circus act that Dachel & I have put on. I lay behind her & press my penis against her listening to the sound of rain. The rain cradles us to sleep.

I have a theory,

-Maybe I am prolonging this because I hate to converse with my father.

-Maybe I am prolonging this because I actually still love Dachel.

-Maybe I am prolonging this because I need to feel close to someone of the opposite sex.

I feel like I have not actually interacted with any real girl besides my mother or the female junkies who know me as the lookout kid.

As we drift off to sleep, Dachel preaches, "I miss you & I only want you. Take this pussy it's all yours. Ever since Rico died, I feel like I need another presence in this house so please move in with me."

Dachel works as a legal secretary for this law firm downtown. She lives in her house due to vouchers from the state of Maryland for low-income individuals. I assume she worked something out with her job in order to be able to have an affordable living situation. I will never ask though, as it's not my place nor my business.

I wake up some 4 hours later realizing that it is pouring down. She is still asleep, but I roll her over to kiss her belly ring until she opens her legs willingly. I then long stroke her getting into repetitive motion. This time, I get into a little pattern of switching the strokes up to moving my dick side to side.

I am determined to make her bust this time & I succeed. She moans loud & her legs quiver while she falls back to sleep.

Finally, I can brag on my performance. Take a bow young fella. I get dressed & skate. Man I ain't nothing but a dog. But she's a bone. I'm just playing my role.

Trenches

Good Fellas

It has died down a bit on Lafayette during the spring because of the rain. Not only is the drug-dealing slow because of the weather, but a few of the main trappers were pinched.

Terrance, Lawrence & Lewis were hemmed up by the K-9 unit a few days ago. I spoke to Whoo who informed me," the grid is down my nigga. Basically no communications by walkies or nothing for a while. It's getting too hot around here. Plus with that nigga Freddie getting murked, cops have been round nonstop."

Even Rell knew to lay low, so he did not investigate the scene any longer. He knows what it is.

Whoo has to go out of state to get a lick because he is not making nearly as much money as he can when the block is booming. It is not like he can hit West North Ave & sling over there. There's a very different dynamic of the multiple areas in Baltimore. East, West & South are those areas you did not just intrude on, that's the law.

Drug dealing is truly a fickle business. Every once in a while, we will get a junkie who wants percs. Shit slow money is the same as no money but niggas went out and got that slow money.

The man George comes around regularly to get whatever can get him high. He comes at least 3 times a day & makes sure that he pays on Fridays because those are the days his direct deposit drops. He is a functioning addict & the only junkie that is allowed a front on the goods.

For some reason he has been MIA after his last purchase. It is getting old waiting around for him, so we continue to focus on other promising sales. None of which I am immediately involved in. I am not a stick-up kid. I definitely will not involve in home invasions.

Besides the drought, Whoo is still eating. The team on the other hand is starving. I am down to 10$ a day fucking with them & since we cannot use walkies, my ass really not getting a dime. Oh well, I still have the stash from when John robbed me. It is the big pot too! Plus I still have leftover money from robbing Rell. I made out good, I was not struggling at all. But the motto is still Get Money!

"If only I could do something with these Acura keys shit." I think to myself. They are my trophy. I robbed one of East Baltimore's notorious hitters. These are bragging rights that I am careful not to brag about.

I make my way to Dachel's house where she tops me off, & then I make my way to Paul's. Paul became a good friend. He has so much information & knowledge of what drug dealing is. He is more like a big brother.

He kind of reminds me of Paulie from Good Fellas. He is always calm & gives accurate advice. In another life, he could have been an activist, but instead he is selling drugs & reminiscing on all of the chicks he used to smash on the strength of him playing ball.

"What's going on Paul, what's the word?
Paul lives on Lanvale Street which is the next street over from mine. It goes North Avenue, Lafayette, & then Lanvale. Each street leads into Hartford road.

Paul is maybe 3 years older than I. He had a basketball scholarship to UMES but fucked it up when he messed up his knee. Every once in a while, he will do a semester there online just to keep his mind sharp.

"Ain't shit what's up Rob?"

"Man not much relaxing trying to figure out how to get some more bread." I gesture while holding Rell's Acura keys.

"Oh shit you still have those?" Paul asks.

"Yea I ain't found out what to do with them bitches yet."

"Man we could jack his shit & then take it to the chop shop down by where the Mexicans live."
The idea is a bold one. It is adding insult to injury, but I do not care because if Rell wanted money, he will do a lot worse than that.

Paul continues, "But between me & you, a lot of us are tired of Whoo & his fucked up mismanagement. He's eating regardless but he ain't sharing shit. Sometimes I wanna take the burner to his head myself."

"For real?! Shit how many other niggas feel like that?" I ask.

"Enough! I mean shit I need money for these classes, I am the only one out here going pay for them." He complains.
"I feel you bro. But let's talk about this Rell situation first. How much you think we can make from the Mexicans?"

"Probably like 5 grand, I guess. It's an older model, right?" Paul guesses.

"True-true, I guess we should make that trip down da hill huh?"

"Yea but we might need the car in one piece if we expect this plan to work ya dig? I have some thinking to do if we expect this thing to go over smoothly & benefit everyone. You are going be hearing from me, & if you don't, just come knock on my door, you know where I stay."
Diabolical
....brains & balls, what finesse!

Trenches

Juice

It seems as if everything is getting under my skin. Even though I have avoided my dad, he still ends up giving me a discussion.

"Robert your mom is concerned that the people you have been hanging with don't have you're best interests in mind. I don't want you out there with those hoodlums fucking up your freedom you hear me? You won't be staying under this roof with this bullshit"

"Dad I hear you, but you know how ma is. She worries about everything & you're not here, so you don't see what's going on. Most of the time we are hooping, and the majority don't sell drugs." I defend.

I'm telling half-truths I mean a lot of them aren't selling drugs but are lookout kids. He is never home so how the hell would he know.

I'm sitting on the front steps sipping on a blue juice from the corner store. The same cops that approached Marlon & I some time ago, drive through nodding his head in respect. I find myself doing nothing but complaining about everything. Frustration kicks in as I found myself battling who I was & who I think I should. I am very impressionable. One day I want to be a drug dealer the next I want to be a geek.

Most of the guys around me are frustrated about money. I am well off though. I participate as if I am struggling as well just to fit in with the overall narrative.

"What's up Rob? How are you feeling?" C.J asks as he, Buggy, Porter & Brice pull up on bikes.

"What's the moves this week Rob?" Buggy asks.

I am amazed at how over the last few months I blend in with the people I used to observe.

"I can't call it fellas," I reply.

Marlon walks down the steps & opens the front door searching for me.

"What you doing Robby?

"Hanging with the fellas we have some shit to take care of," I reply.

"Cool I'm trying fuck with y'all." Marlon smiles.

I give Marlon this look of contempt. It wasn't that I do not want him around, I just did not want to mix him up with all of the bullshit. I went from a college kid out to a product of my environment in a matter of just over a year. I have been progressively more involved in illegal activities. It has been times we have run down on junkies who owed up. I never did anything except watch them beat up people who never pay drugs.

I don't know how far we will go today, so I have to keep Marlon pure as far away from my antics as possible. It was way easy for me to be peer pressured into this kind of life, & to me, it feels like I inherited that part from Rico.

"Uh never mind," Marlon replies as he walks back into the house defeated.

"Didn't that junkie George owe us money though? We saw him on the 1400 block shordy lets bust a move on that ass!" Brice convinces.

"Aight bet that!" I shrug.

Porter, Buggy, Brice, C.J & I ride three bikes across the block on the other side of the projects to where we know George is probably scoping out houses looking for anything he can steal & pawn. Brice who is usually as quiet as a mouse is first to spot him but points him out. "There goes that bitch ass nigga right there!"

Once we get within striking distance, I rock him directly in his jaw. The force of my hand against his jawbone is like me trying to break through a reinforced door with my shoulder, everything moved except the door.

I don't know if it is peer pressure or built-up tension from Whoo that makes me savagely attack George. It is uncharacteristically unlike me to harm anyone innocent or who did not have it coming. Besides it's not like he owes me money. None of that matters in that veil of destruction & misdirection as we wail on George for no apparent reason but to become every negative stereotype that we viewed in those black movies about the hood. I grew into the archetype that Marlon & I loathe.

We all surround George so that he has no chance to square up with any of us. I kick George in the ribs, Buggy jabs him in his chest, & C.J kicks him in his gut. After a while, we all stop using our fists.

Porter lifts George's chin & taunts him with the blade he bought from the BP gas station and says, "Next time you owe that cake you better pay it or end up on the 5:00 news." It's almost as identical to a movie scene. Brice picks up a trash can that is unusually full because today happens to be trash day & tosses it on old man George in the worse, demeaning way possible.

"Fuck y'all! All y'all better respect me. I'm a war vet. Y'all think y'all are above respect." George replies.

"Ay yo stomp his shit!" C.J rallies.

"Help! Help! Help!" George yells as we continue beating him.

I catch a resident peek through their window blinds, but it does not deter me. I am part of the in-crowd, which I never have been. We are stupid & young because we did this in pure daylight.

WHOOP WHOOP

Suddenly & swiftly, the police swerve in front of us, they hop out & swing Buggy on his face. I knew instantly that he probably cracked a few teeth. I hop on the bike as fast as I can & turn right onto Caroline Street. I catch a glimpse of Brice shaking the other fat officer & laugh to myself. These are my guys!

We all escape except for Buggy. We assume the officers probably took him to baby bookings downtown. He is only 16 so they will probably let him off easy. Plus George will not snitch because he still needs his fix. He is a functioning addict after all. George is a veteran who works at Franklin Square Hospital as a Janitor. His schedule is religious. Up at 5 am and back by 6 pm. He will still come up with the money & then some for his next hit of coke. Buggy is just the collateral damage that happened in the process.

Buggy is the hardest 16-year-old I know. He is small but has heart, it's just in the wrong place though. Even I know he could be doing more productive things with his energy, yet I have little man following me. Buggy has an olive complexion. He is dark skin with trashy "hood" tattoos. His nose is wide & his grin made all of the girls go nuts over him. He always brags about losing his virginity at 12 years old.

87

Buggy looks up to me as an older brother. I do not need it though, because I have a younger brother. Marlon is just out busy obtaining his education.

We meet back at my house & chill on the stoop. The same cop that gave me a head nod earlier drives through with a different type of energy on his face. The kid he once regarded is the one that is around the same individuals who I am said to be more mature than.
It doesn't matter though because the hood's motto will forever be "Fuck the cops".

"Man this summer is live as shit already!" C.J exclaims.

We did not care if the police look for us, we know George will not give our government. We all agree on that.

Hours later we see Buggy getting out his mama's van she is ignorant of the fact that we are a bad influence on him.

"Yo Buggy!!! My nigga" we celebrate.

"What you sipping on my nigga?"

"Got that strong." He replies as he squeezes his Capri-sun juice pouch.

"Aye! Ha-ha." Porter laughs.

Juice sounds like love right about now. Paul & I know that Whoo has the juice, but he doesn't know I'm coming for it.

I cannot wait until he gets back into town.

Trenches

Veni, Vidi, Vici

BOOM! BOOM!

There is only smoke & the smell of gun powder. We race to the top floor of the three-story Asquith Street home. We know the goal, the mission, plus the prize. This is war!

Porter, Leonard, Freaky, & Hammond are with me on this little "expedition". On our way up we run into a few guys we know from prior visits. The 2 guys always posted outside are the first to go down in a bloody massacre. I was ill-prepared for this onslaught. I pretty much let everyone else do the conscious-heavy work. I do not think I will be able to sleep with the images of pure murder.

"To your left Hammond!" Freaky points multiple targets out clearing the steps and rooms as we raid at night.

Hammond lets loose. "Uhhhhhhhh!" He hits a shadow with a headshot. That smith & Wesson came in handy. Hammond's a sharpshooter. He used to brag about before his grandfather died, he would always take him to the gun range. His veteran status brought him favor with many of the vendors there.

"Freaky! Freaky! Watch the fucking sides!" Freaky shoots a dude from relatively short range in the back as he runs away from the chaos.

We all wear black skully masks because that's all we know. We watched every urban movie & agreed that we needed some equipment. We receive most of the guns from the hippy weed selling crackheads girlfriend. We know she would comply, not to mention we bartered with her.
Crack rocks for some weapons. "Fairtrade aunty?" I asked as I thought back to the transaction. She was more than willing to help, seeing that she no longer had a breadwinner to score her any more drugs. Not to mention Whoo is the direct reason her crackhead boyfriend is locked in prison.

Leonard takes point as we make it to the top floor. We spread out making sure there are no more enemies in the rooms. We clear each room in pairs. Each room except the main one.

"Leonard kick that bitch in!" I holler.

 Where them hands man!? Let me see em!

"Don't fucking move" Hammond yells.

"Freaky get the tape bruh." It's time to break him."
"Aight I'm cool. I'm cool." Whoo replies as we begin to wrap him up.

He looks frightened as if we appear like ghosts. He never in a million years expected me to dump on him the way he has been dumping on our neighborhood for years.

I'm sure he just got back in town from making moves, so he definitely is a bit disoriented and exhausted. Perfect timing.

I slowly lift my mask to reveal my face. "Not what you were expecting huh?!" The fear on his face subsides because he still characterizes me as this timid petrified kid. I am a militant strategist with one goal in mind.

Operation: Take Back Our Hood

"Shordy tell me this a joke." Whoo laughs confidently. He did the kind of laugh that you shrug someone off with. His fear turns into pure entertainment at our expense. I was not going to give him the satisfaction though.

I hate when people act nonchalant but Whoo is oblivious to that fact. I pull out the taser from my cargo pants pocket & press it to his chest. "What's the combination to the safe Whoo?" I ask.

"I should have let Rico kill you. I should have fucked Dachel harder! I should have buried your lor brother!" Whoo snaps.

"Leonard grab that water bottle on the dresser," I instruct.

Whoo has been smoking which is evident from the smell. He is high as hell. I wonder if he even heard us role up & shoot the two guys he's always with, Dillon & Jason out front.

I grab the water bottle from Leonard and pour it on Whoo. "If I put this taser to your chest, you will light the fuck up! What's the code?"

"33, 17, 50!" Whoo gives me the code with the quickness. "Ok you have the code plus the stash, but how are you going to stay alive when this is all through?" He asks.

Hammond laughs followed by Freaky. Leonard & I keep a stoic face. I look around Whoo's room. It's beige & aged. The paint is chipped & there is a pot in the corner where the sheetrock is corroded due to the ceiling leaking. There are magazines scattered & Xbox games all over the floor of his room. The floor is brown and wooden, but bare.

There is no carpet & the windows have mismatched drapes on each. As far as I could see, he can only see out of the side because it only has two windows which are partially a reason, he needs multiple lookouts. Much of his view is obscured. There is also a light with a fan fixture attached to it. The light bulb is visible, with many mosquitoes tantalized by the glow.

He is actually living here. He broke the rule, never sell or make the product where you lay your head.

"I don't think you get it Whoo. There will be no retaliation."

Freaky hands me his burner, & I attached the scorpion stinger on it. I do that just for dramatics.

I lean in a bit & repeat his confident line, "it's nothing that can't be ironed out." This narcissist is finally tasting real fear.

Trenches

Closing Up Shop

I call Paul on the phone. "Everything is straight," Paul says. "Aight cool roll through its going be done in like 5 mins," I inform him.

"Cool!"

I hang the phone up & wait until I see Paul pull up in like 10 minutes. Got damn that boy is punctual.

Paul steps outside of Kirk's red Ford Taurus in his all black with the face mask rolled on top of
his head. He makes his way through the carnage.

"What's up fellas?" Asks Paul as he steps into the main room. "Damn y'all did a bang-up ass job downstairs shorty."

We are all hustlers, tired of getting a small percentage of the pie that Whoo elects for us. Well at least they are. I am just happy to dethrone him for all of his forced coercion & manipulation.

"You too?! Paul I would have never lumped you in with these fuck boys. The only loyal nigga left I have is Kirk." Whoo protests.

"Shit Kirk was my first stop" Paul brags. "I had tried to persuade him to come on to our side & shit. I asked him if he wanna make some real dough? But like you said he was too loyal. Now Unc sitting on the couch with his top chopped off."

Loose end number 1 tied.

I had not even accounted for Kirk. I would love to have taken him out a long time ago personally. He had a big ego, but now that ego is peeled back...literally.

"Aight y'all finish up here, Imma go ahead & call up Rell's homeboy using his phone and tell him I know who robbed him," Paul commands.

"Yeah on Lafayette hurry I got em up here." I hear Paul's voice echo in the background.
He calls one of the numbers that's saved in the iPhone I took when I robbed Rell. He didn't know which number corresponded to Rell's homeboy, so he just called the most frequently used one.

"They are going to be here shortly."

"Damn Whoo. You should have cut everyone in. You managed to trash the entire community. You wanted loyalty but are the most disloyal of all.

"Freaky?! Hammond?! I fed y'all don't follow this clown! I'm the one who put him on. Y'all my dawgs!" Whoo pleads.

"For every time you threatened Marlon…Fuck you!"

Blickup Blickup!

Two shots in the head rotate his chair as his lifeless body hits the floor. His face bruises from where the bullet enters his temple.

It's my second murder, & even though it did not get any easier, this one is therapeutic.

Loose end number 2 tied.

Rell pulls up in his Acura. He runs through the "empire" with 4 niggas & makes his way to Whoo's room. Shit if I was him, I would have stopped at the first dead nigga on the steps, but he probably thinks the person that called him did it & has his opponent upstairs hemmed up.

But we would not know because we have already dipped out of the obscured backside of the building.

I left him a treat though. I opened the coke room & let the ammonia smell seep up the steps. I doused the whole upstairs with ammonia & bleach destroying whatever evidence of our presence I can. We also make sure the fan is turned so that it blows inside instead of out. Shit was clever too; it can help to disorient them as well as provide more of a mystery for the police to figure out.

*In a low voice on a phone

"Baltimore police we've already sent officers in the area.
Hello, hello?"

****

"Yo wtf?!" Rell says as he enters Whoo's room & hears a voice on his cellphone. "Yo check his pockets!"

"Yo I know ole boy. I did a bid with him way back." Rell continues.

One of his boys checks the pockets & pulls out Rell's keys, along with his cell phone. The phone has 911 on it & the call has been going on for about 25 minutes. They have officers already in pursuit.

"Oh shit! Book it!"

Whoop Whoop!

Just in time the Baltimore cops surround the building with helicopters above. The swat team touches down first because of the nature of the call. Too many of the residents heard all of the gunshots & are making multiple anonymous calls. What a hell of a night.

Loose end number 3 tied & burned.

Fleeting Peace

It is relatively quiet lately. I told Paul, "take all the drugs that you got from Whoo & sell em but make sure all the money you got out that safe you split it up with the fellas. I do not want any parts of it fam, I'm pretty much done with that bullshit."

"Aight cool. You sure you don't want a cut of this Rob I mean shit we tag-teamed the whole Eastside." Paul laughs.

"Nigga I'm positive." I laugh out loud.

"Make sure you keep your nose clean boy, you too smart to be out here dealing with this bullshit."

"Yea Imma bust a move & sell it to some white boys down South in Brooklyn, then I'm done. I'm thinking about going back to school for good. Man you should come to UMES with me though!"

"Shit sounds good to me," I reply.

I know I cannot afford it but damn if it didn't sound nice. Out of pocket money for an A1 school... I do not think it is in the cards for that.

I salute the fellas as I walk back to my house with my hands in my pants holding my crouch. Shit we went through a tour in Afghanistan in my mind. I tied up a few loose ends but still have a couple that clouds my mind. Later that day I catch the bus to the cemetery.

"Ay what's up bro? Hope you up there keeping me safe man. Your life meant something, I just wanted to let you know." I begin to grin and laugh, "yo you remember that time we let Mr. Grady's dogs out his gate & he came outside with his belt in his hand, yo his pants were falling."
I burst out laughing...... We were a regular Dennis the Menace duo. Just a little bit of mischief.
I cannot find the tears that I wanted. When you cry, all of the emotions deep down seep out, which helps relax the mind.

In my mind, even though Rico betrayed me, it never appeases my conscience to think "an eye for an eye. I mean how could it? Killing Rico was a domino effect that spiraled my life into one filled with regret, fear & sorrow.

I know what I should do.

I call up Dachel with trembling frustration & fear, I ask, "baby are you busy?"

"No I'm free Hun, you coming by today?" She replies.

We decided to be a couple, but it is more of friends with benefits situation than a relationship. I visit her when I want affection because it is the only thing, she can offer me. I offer her company as it is the least I could do since removing Rico from her life.

"Yea Imma make my way to you in a bit love."

The bus drive is long but only because I have not rehearsed what I want to say. I arrive outside of Dachel's brown door at a reasonable time. I enter with the spare key that she provided me with.

"Dachel!" I holler.

She descends the steps slowly in my mind, but in reality, she is moving at a normal pace. I guide her to the kitchen where I pull out a chair for her adorned with gold trim.
"Damn, baby it's going to hurt you to hear this......."

Trenches

Tears in the Bucket

"**W**hat the fuck you mean you killed him?! No, no, no, unacceptable. You supposed to be his best fucking friend yo!"

I can do no wrong in Dachel's eyes, but this is an exception, as it should be.

"Yo did you listen to anything I said?! Whoo told me to kill him or it was my ass & Marlon's. Man & not only that but Rico was going to kill me! I know you miss your cousin, but it was survival!"

I am instantly defensive even though I am not in the wrong. An old proverb once said, "never argue with a woman, you will never win." I look around the kitchen. There is brown wood paneling on the walls with a cream-colored tile decorating the floor which is most likely oak under it. This house has been here a long time, but somehow Dachel managed to make it a beautiful home as well as keep up the maintenance.

"If I could take it back I damn sure would love, you know how it is to make bad decisions!" I go on the offensive.

"Oh so now this is about me fucking Whoo huh?! You know what get the fuck out! And leave Ya key nigga.!"

...."You lucky I don't call the cops on ya bitch ass! Bitch ass nigga! Bitch ass nigga! Get the fuck outta here you ain't no real nigga!"

I throw my hands in the air, & just walk out. I slam the front door in my departure.

BOW!

The further I walked from her house, the less turmoil & grieving I hear. I hope she is not considering telling the cops what I told her, shit the deeds are already fucking done. I make sure I only tell her about the first incident involving Whoo, Rico & I.

I always said I would lose her if I ever told her & this was evident. The truth hurts, no matter how you cut it. I clear my conscience & push another person away. At least confessing gives me the realization that I have at least some respect for Dachel. It may not have been much, but shit would you tell someone you don't fuck with incriminating information.

"Fuck this shit." I walk around the corner & stop at a sign by Ark Baptist church. It reads,
"DON'T WAIT UNTIL ITS TOO LATE TO ASK FOR FORGIVENESS"

Shit I thought about walking in those doors & confessing, but I know that is unnecessary. I'll just go home, shut my door & say 5 Hail Mary's.

Shit I wonder how long it took Judas' guilt to break him before he killed himself.
Meh just a thought.

Trenches

Déjà vu

I wake up earlier than usual today. I pull the covers off & walk into the bathroom to wash my face. I yawn the entire walk while bouncing off of the narrow walls of the dark upstairs hallway. Everything seems okay, but then again it feels the opposite. I feel as if I am truly missing something. Is it Dachel? Is it Rico? Is it drug money? Is it God?

So many questions run through my mind early as I brush my teeth & peer into the smudged filthy bathroom mirror. Then I ask myself, "who am I?"

I walk into Marlon's room & catch a glimpse of him filling out job applications.
"Fuck you doing up so early?" He greets.

"I don't know I can't sleep, really I can't stay asleep, I kept tossing & waking up all night. I know I had a few nightmares, but I can only remember bits & pieces of them. Shit still doesn't make any sense."

"Still ain't talk to Dachel yet? I know you miss her." Marlon replies with a slick smirk.
"I do but I don't. I miss the pussy of course, but my pride won't let me hit her up. Besides she the one who kicked me out. I can give two fucks

at the moment but I'm sure later down the line we both will come around."

"True. True."

"What about you why you up so early? You playing with yourself?" I joke.

"You funny, nah I'm looking for jobs that kind of deal with my major at school. If I can find a technical job that will groom me, then see Ya. I wouldn't even mind moving to Florida for real. I heard housing down there is cheaper."

"Florida sounds like a good move. All the women you can ask for plus you can cop the most recent jays or dopes." I agree.

"True shit. I'm hungry as shit though. You think our parents went to the market?"

"You mean El Cheapo? Man hell no we are going have to find our food as usual. Trying walk to McDonald's?"

"Yea why not."

It is just like old times. Just us before everyone became more comfortable with us at 1300. I kind of miss it. That feeling of talking to someone else who knows & goes through the same strife as myself.

We get dressed making sure we look presentable in case we run into some girls. We make our way through the alley cutting through section 8 houses behind ours. McDonald's is not far at all. Maybe about a 7-minute walk, granted you do not get hit trying to cross busy ass North Avenue.

I order a double cheeseburger from the nice looking burgundy haired girl from the 2nd register & laugh as Marlon's order is taken by a crunchy black older woman with the yellow sclera. She is polite just not appealing for a nineteen and twenty-year-old.

I flirted with my cashier to make my face known to her as I would be regularly visiting just to see her. I read her name tag; her name is Vanessa. Pretty.

She is hip to my flirtatious nature as she responds, " you know, we're still serving breakfast, right?!"

Mc Donald's employees remain undefeated!

"Well, let me get a hot cake platter please & thank you." I quip.

We take the same way home pass the courthouse on Hartford road smashing our hash browns & geek about the employees of

McDonald's. We make it back at the same dirty alley filled with smashed rats & dog feces.

I see someone that looks familiar.

 "Hold up Marlon, I know him."

I recognize the man as none other than backstabbing John, shooting up. I approach him.

"Yo wassup, wassup Robby baby?" Let me get some fries or something, my nigga."
I laugh at the thought of me helping someone who robbed me, but I consider it. Besides it is a new day.

"Here you go my brother; you take it easy." I relinquish a piece of my hash brown.

"Whose that?" Marlon asks.

We walk home with me enlightening Marlon on our prior history. John probably does not even remember me, but I forgive him. There is no need to linger in the past.

Trenches

Due Process

Freaky, Leonard, Hammond, Paul, Porter & I sit on the concrete wall on the basketball court. Freaky & Porter pass a blunt back & forth. I back up each time they pass it between one another.

"Y'all killing me with that smoke."

I get up to hop in the game of "Fifty" that Marlon is winning. That's the reason Freaky, Leonard,

Hammond, & Porter are sitting on the sideline. He put them all out with a deep 3-point jumper.
Paul is playing but periodically hopping out the game to check on the block. He still has his hands in drug dealing. I do not think he is interested in enrolling for classes, but what do I know?
Paul jumps back in the game after checking Lafayette for the knockers. He goes for a lay-up against Marlon & cashes the bucket. He has already "broke the ice."

"Damn Marlon you let this nigga jump in the game & put you out?"

"Chill nigga cause he about to do the same to you," Marlon replies.

Marlon has become somewhat of a threat on the court with his awkward & unpredictable ball-handling skills, but none on the block could rival Paul. Hand down, man down!

"Check." I check the ball, soon as it bounces back into Paul's hands, he shoots a perfect form jumper cashing it in.

Everyone on the sideline goes nuts. "Damn. He did your dumb ass. Paul shot wet."

I brush off the consigning & observe Buggy limping to the court. Buggy has this funny walk. Like he has just gotten off of work or something. Each time he arrives, the fellas would smirk because no young person should walk like they are in pain.

We later find out he has a degenerative disorder; I believe it's a form of arthritis. His hip bone & socket rub against one another with no cushion. After that, we never really smirked at it.

"Waddup with y'all?

"Ain't shit waddup boy?" Replies Leonard.

"Nothing just got word your boy out on bail."

"Who?"

"Rell. He just posted bail. You know my mother works as a correctional officer."

"Damn shit I hope he pleads out and takes that L," I reply.

"Or are we going have to bury his ass?" Paul snickers.

Marlon who is hip to everything that has transpired chimes in. " Y'all are missing the point. Even if he does go to trial or pleas, he can still bailout. It's not a matter of them holding him because eventually, he has to go back to court. It is about what he does while he's out."

Deep! I never knew Marlon was a CSI: Baltimore fan I joke inside. But he has a point.

Paul is accustomed to this lifestyle. Another murder to him will just put another body under his belt. He & John were beefing because John kept asking for money to feed his addiction. Paul was threatening to off him, so I know what he is saying about Rell is true. If karma comes around, I will have no choice.

I am not ready to step back into this degree of things. I found pleasure in just hooping & conversing with my brother. The sad truth is that if Rell is in fact out on bail with any info of who we are, he will put a hit out on us before he even makes it to court. Jail is nothing to him, revenge is everything.

This relative peace for me has been rejuvenating. I have my best friend Marlon back, along with the guys around me who used to always turn their noses up at us. It is a bit perplexing to believe that at one point in time, they wanted to beat us down just because. Now as I see things up close, I see more & more how similar we all are.

Take Porter for an example. Porter is a brown-skinned 24-year-old with a lean build but has a wide wingspan. He can palm a basketball with ease. His jumper is terrible, but when he drives to the baseline, he always makes the layup. Porter has tattoos on his face & hands. One reads "Crip 4 Life." To be honest, you would think because of his tattoos that he is some kind of high-strung thug, but he is a chilled back relaxed individual. He has no parents but lives with his baby moms 3 doors down from us.

Freaky is known for his influence with the neighborhood women. Every day he tells tales of his exploits, & he is never shy of the details. He once showed us a video of a girl who happened to walk past us that very day. No one looks at her the same. Freaky is brown-skinned as well & a bit shorter than Porter but is also a bit heavier. He wears it well plus the more he hoops, the slimmer he seems to get.

Leonard & Hammond are twins. Both light-skinned with tats covering each arm. They like freaky get all of the girls as well. They always showed love before I was popping so I never really viewed them as enemies. They just had great ties to the other people who didn't care for my family. Leonard & Hammond are both tall & slinky with cruddy temps. You can only tell them apart by their tattoos. Weirdly, their parents did not name them something that typically coincided with their "twindom". Something on the lines of Leonard & Kennard, or Hammond & Howard would have sufficed.

I am accustomed to the life of being the heart of my neighborhood. Everyone is pretty much a homeboy. We reconciled those petty differences that drove us to hate one another which is an excellent slice of heaven. It used to be bad enough being picked on in school, then coming home and have to be on edge. Now it is love and brotherhood. But at what cost! On our block, there is not too much news about black on black crime, just a lot of drug crime that the news ostracized to feed their agenda. I know eventually, the police will install a blue box for surveillance.

The blue boxes are a box screwed to a light pole that blinked blue light. I have no idea if it is to signify that this is a bad area that needs to be policed, or of it is a camera that the police installed to deter anyone from crime. I have not even seen any of these in other states....just Baltimore City. That should paint a picture.

You know, paint the image of the typical black everyday youth as gangsters which we are by the way, but they do not know why we are that way. It is not fair to come with a preconceived notion or characterization on people you do not understand. I mean that's 99% of the reason us guys never got along.

Nonetheless I think media is the furthest thing from my mind. Every time I believe myself to be progressing, the finish line stretches further away from me. I am losing my grip. This anxiety, pressure and fear are not good for my soul.

Damn here we go with this riff-raff again. I thought when I took up praying, shit like this stops happening. Shit I just need God to have my back one last time, then I can stop praying & continue living my sinful life.

How ironic that I admit these thoughts to myself as if God cannot read my mind...

......I'm a trip.

Trenches

Rell's Point of View

Shit, I been locked down for a couple of months now. Maybe a month or 2 I don't know, as time seems to sit still when you in a holding cell. This ain't new to me though. I been in the system, I beat the system. I come in & go out like it is a revolving door. Dude who robbed me must have set me up, but when I find him, Imma rock his ass. I been plotting this since getting booked. He just made an enemy he can't afford. I don't know why lor yo been trying to get at me. Maybe I fucked his bitch or robbed his peep. Imma get it popping. I must have been in the right area looking for his bitch ass cause all of a sudden, my shit starts turning up, & I don't believe in coincidences.

Imma keep it a buck, anyone who wants me to lay down going have to get down, cause It won't be that easy, I mean its "Bmore". Too much money to be made, & Imma get mine. These niggaz ain't trying to get paid, they trying to get sprayed.

Shordy really called the boys on me though. That's snitching shit, he can't be a street nigga cause he broke the code. Jail is a worse punishment than death. They trying to charge me with murder, money laundering, distribution & manufacturing of narcotics. The cops know I ain't do that shit that's why this next bail hearing, my lawyer assured me I should be able to go home. I am way more aggravated at being accused of shit I know I ain't have no parts in, compared to getting off and being guilty. I need to be found innocent of all charges so I can be guilty of them later on when I catch the slick nigga who set me up. I'm not even going rob his ass. I just wanna know our connection & leave his ass on the corner leaking.

Man I do this shit & have managed to keep myself from being jammed up. What is even more fucked up is I don't know where they have my homies at.

I'm lucky I have the bread for a good lawyer. A Jewish dude named Richard Goldstein shit he got me off the first time I got knocked. I have always stacked bread. Hopefully he can get me some lesser charges. I don't know which charges will stick or which will fold. When you have a convicted felon like me being accused of major drug offenses, it alarms the judge before you even see his or her face. But when you have a convicted felon accused of murder, it's like the judge sees your evolution from a petty non-compliant drug dealer to a hitman.

 I don't know if I have much faith in Rich but I'm hoping he can make sum shake. My prior criminal past is sure to connect a few dots. Especially when one of the deceased is someone, I was in lock-up with. " Terrell Jenkins, you just posted bail."

The hearing went well. I mean I made bail but still am facing a shitload of different charges. I think that nigga Rich gotta be fucking the DA or someone because they lowered my bond Significantly.

"MY WHITEBOY."

I already knew I would make bail this time, I'm just glad it cost less than it initially was. My second hearing ain't until 3 months down the line, but before then, a nigga gotta find out who killed shordy & why they attached my name to that shit. The streets will talk though it's only a matter of time. I just have to squeeze the information out of it as I did with that other situation.

It was June 15th, 2012. One of my lor cousins had been walking in Sandown early in the morning to catch the bus to work. He worked at the Marriott at the Inner Harbor. He was about 19 at the time & early in the morning it is pretty dark when you have to be at the bus stop at 5 am.

Some dude walks up to him and asked," yo what time it is?"
My cousin was green. He wasn't all in like me. He reached for his pocket & took his phone out of his pocket, checked, & right at that moment, I knew he probably realized the setup before it rolled out.

"It's 4:forty........."
Before he knew it, he had been stabbed in his spleen, and all he saw was a man running away with his phone.

My cousin Derrick was laying in the middle of the concrete sidewalk with blood oozing out that he couldn't plug. I wish I could say it was a life lesson, but it wasn't. I mean when I think about it, I've robbed nigga at gunpoint & even shot them after I ran them out of everything they had. I never watch the news, but I knew some of my victims died. It's funny how I can be angry as fuck for someone robbing my cousin but turn around & do the same shit to someone's father, uncle, nephew or son.

My cousin told me everything that happened while in the hospital, & I was going to let it go & say fuck it if it wasn't for him passing the next morning after. They told me that he was good after we talked when he was alert. Said the hole was patched & everything but that morning when he wasn't responsive, they turned him & found the bed sheets soaked with blood and plasma. That shit shook me.

I went to where he was stabbed in the sprinter that night. I knew someone had seen something. There was a small vigil going on with his homeboy in charge. I pulled him up right away.
"Ay yo, Terry what type of phone Derrick had?" I ask.
"Uh he had an iPhone, why you ask?" Derrick replies.
"You good with technology & shit, right? Yea that's what I'm in school for."
"Aight bet I need you to do me a favor, I have Derrick's computer right here somebody said you could use it to find iPhones or some shit like that, I don't know how to do all of that, but I need that asap."

Now that I think about it, I should have had ole boy do the same thing for my iPhone that shordy up North Ave took from me.

"You ain't tell the police?"

"Nigga do it look like I'm waiting on the police to handle this? That's my cousin, that's blood, fuck the cops. Handle that right here!"

I must of shook shordy because he had the information in 3 minutes tops. The tracker or whatever it was lead me to an address that was an abandoned or condemned home. I cut through the front where the no trespassing sign was hanging on by 1 screw.
I see 2 junkies sitting on the floor with a pile of phones next to them. Each one smashed except for Derricks. I'm assuming they know that the phones can be tracked & deliberately smashed them. I don't know why they didn't smash Derricks. Both junkies had been freebasing crack & were out of it. I didn't even say any words. I waited to come back the next night. I wanted them to feel the pain & I knew they would be too numb to have these bullets go through the back of their brains.

The next night sure enough, I went to the same place & didn't waste a breath trying to ask questions or see if they were the culprits. I just aimed & fired. I shot her in the eye, & I made sure I shot him in his face a few times until he was unrecognizable...
"Keep the phone."

....
..

"Can I use your phone?"

I need to call my man's Moodah so he can scoop me up. Shit they had me separated from the rest of my fellas so I can't even connect with them & see if they made bail. Fuck it, one problem at a time.

"Yo Moodah, it's Rell boy pick me up I'm down bookings."

"Already, your muva told me you were getting out. I got you, hold still I will be there with Toya & Smitty."

"Bet."

20 mins later.......

"My nigga what' sup?"

"Man nothing glad I'm out for real. You think you can drop me up old boy way, you know they still got my car & shit."

"Why you ain't tell me? I'd a got it for you." Toya asks.
"Cause dummy, it's not in your name it's in his muva name they can't let just anybody pick up shit," Smitty replies.

"True but on the real, you lucky they held it so long. I'm surprised they didn't auction that bitch off." Moodah replies.

I suck my teeth. "Man that's probably because they looking to connect it to the case. Probably looking for fingerprints & shit. I don't know. That bitch clean I paid straight-up cash & put it in my muva name so they wouldn't suspect nothing."

"Yea that's true. Arad so where dude that you found dead stay?" Moodah asks.
"He stays up over east by North Ave, right? Off one of the side streets & shit." Toya confirms.
Moodah pulls off as his memory comes back to him. I direct him to where I used to come down Aiken looking for the kid that robbed & shot me.

"Ay yo, pull up in that back alley bruh. Imma see what that junky knows."
I roll the window down inconspicuously trying not to ruffle any more feathers of law enforcement.

"Aye, Unc let me holler at you!"

John walks over steadily stumbling over the trash he's been taking from the trashcan.

"Waddup, you got something to eat. I ain't ate all day?"

"That's cause you prioritize the wrong shit G. Aye you know who was beefing with Whoo?"

"Yea, yea the lor nigga that live on the corner. His name Rob."

"Good looking out." I slide him 20$.

Trenches

Karma

Rell posts a quarter mil for his bail, I did not know his money was that long.

On the bright side he has not seen any of our faces except mine, will he remember? He does not know us personally but what I have done to me should be taken very personally.

Still the thought of him attempting anything on my life or my family has me knocking at Paul's door.

Knock Knock

"Who is it?"

"It's Robby, Paul's friend," I announce proudly. Paul's cousin answers the door.

"Hold on. Paul!? You have company."

Paul comes to the door dressed in his gym shorts ready to demolish someone on the court.

"Waddup Bruh?" Paul greets as he daps me up.

"Ain't shit just thinking about the shit we were talking about the other day. About Rell."

"What you think we should take him out? You think he that much of a threat because I can't see him getting out on bail & getting any more potential cases under his belt." Paul replies.

"The nigga did just post hella bread for bail, just throwing that out there. And I'm just trying to double tie & knot this loose end before he comes around screwing shit up." I respond.

"I feel you, walk with me I'm bout to put up some shots."

Paul & I walk to the basketball court to shoot a few shots. He's 9 for 10, as for me, I am 3 for 10.

In the back of my mind I want to talk some more about the situation at hand, but the release of the ball from my wrist is relieving the stress & pressure which allows me to not think about it as much.

By the time Paul leaves, Marlon & I shoot around.

"What's on ya mind Robby?" Marlon asks.

"Right now, just getting away from the hood. It's not like the movies man. It's just not like the movies. I want to be able to have money to get my parents away from here. I want money so I can never have to go back to that stupid shit again. I like to just be free of this without looking over my shoulders anymore."

Marlon snickers.

"Nigga weren't you in school just like me? You let being shot take away that. School is the ticket away from here. Why the fuck you think I left. Do you think I want to come back? Hell no. And guess what soon as I find another internship, I'm leaving again."

"You have a point but...."

"But what? You have no valid excuse! Excuses are tools of incompetence." Marlon quotes.
Each time he uses that quote, it snaps me back to my senses. It always makes me realize how book smart he is & how much my street smarts did not amount to anything. He makes me feel like the little brother. I am a sorry excuse for a role model. Man he is successful without one. It's crazy because I look up to my little brother.

I mean why did I drop out of college? Is it the shooting? Is it depression? It can be a multitude of different things. I was depressed before the shooting, & contemplating trying something new in life. I did not have a plan nor any idea what that would be, but I still wanted to do something. Maybe I could write. Maybe I could write a novel or autobiography who knows. All I know is - I don't know. I pray to God every night to please reveal my gifts, & or talents so that I may use them to give something back to the world. Moms always say, " God has a specific gift for everyone along with a purpose. Everyone is special in their way."

I never saw it. If I prayed for God to give me my gift, which he never delivers, does that make me not special? I mean there are people with multiple gifts, yet I cannot even figure out what I am good at. Sometimes I feel like the black sheep of God's creations or maybe he & his angels are playing cruel jokes on me, no matter, I was losing faith in God's master plans anyhow. I mean look at how far left I must have strayed from "the plan".

I just figure school is not part of it. Depression of losing my best friend along with the issues I faced growing up as a youth does not help me any either. I will have to get myself spiritually & mentally right before I can re-stitch the path I was on before all of this nonsense occurred.

I know one thing, & that's to limit my exposure to Rell or any of this street life. That is 1 option or kill him before he can open the lid on my life & expose the worms that I have been nursing. "He has to be a nonfactor" I convince myself. Marlon & I continue to shoot around simultaneously conversing when someone steps on the court & asks...

" What y'all playing 50? Can I jump in?"

Trenches

Escalation

The air around my body shifts. Goosebumps were born on my brown skin. My hairs stand as if static is in the air. This is that same unwanted feeling as the time I was led to that dingy pee-stained basement.

Rell steps on the court & asks, "can I jump in?"

"It's a free country dug."

I motion for Marlon to chill on the sideline of the court. From my facial expression, Marlon deduces that there is a situation. Trouble always seems to follow me like a shadow. With Marlon around, the circumstances are much more dangerous because now everything on Lafayette affects us. My past has caught up to me....while I'm unprepared no less.

These are the type of situations that make me question if God truly has angels around for protection. Has he forsaken me yet again? My faith wavers in the wind with the rustling of tree branches as the seconds Rell steps on the court converts into an eternity.

I wish I could stay in this eternity forever, but the present is steady gripping me & pulling me back. Time always has a strong grip. Time puts me in a full-Nelson making me relinquish what little control I thought I possessed.

If only my grandma's spirit warned me of this beforehand. This storm of my life is getting even more vicious. The winds are pulling away at my flesh. The rain is washing my blood away from my meat. The cold is freezing my raw heart. I'm dying to live.

"We can play 1on1 if you want," I reply.

Rell smiles with that cruddy look. Even in the light, he still manages to be an apparition of darkness. With the sunlight I can see the tattoos on his face. I have no clue of what they signify or mean.

"Cool, cool, that's what it is then."

I notice a car parked in the alley behind our house. Black tints, I cannot see anyone in it. My parents are home so we must avoid any & all altercations if possible. Though I know that will be unlikely. I am aware of the impending drama & wish I had my ratchet but the last thing I can do is run to my house and grab it, leaving Marlon on the court by himself.

Not to mention no matter what move I make; I will probably be blasted as I attempt to get inside my house. I do not want my parents burying their boys. Especially not Marlon. He is the only innocence left cast off from me. I will not come back from that, well their image of me anyways.

"You Rob?"

"Yea I am he," I reply.

"I got some questions for you my nigga. Trust me you are going wanna hear everything I say. Word is you were the lookout kid for the nigga Whoo. I mean it makes sense because your street has the perfect angle for any cars coming down that aren't known that's pretty genius."

"Where are you getting this information from my nigga?" I quip defensively.

"That ain't important slim. I haven't been up here in a hot minute. You know I came up this way looking for a nigga that shot & robbed me."

"Is that right? Whoo was my mans, & it's fucked up what happened to him." I replied attempting to convince Rell I was shaken by his death.

"That's just the nature of the business. He got caught slipping just as I did that while back. Do you know how many questions I had to answer when I went to the hospital after being shot? Who shot you? Why were you out at night? Did you shoot back? All chitter-chatter that I didn't wanna hear because I knew I didn't care about the police exploring any leads until I had explored them myself. So many questions, especially being shot in the ass. You ever been shot Rob?"

"I had my run-ins with a barrel before, so Where are you going with this Rell?" I reply.

"HAHAHA!" Rell Snickers. "How do you know my name?"

"Same way you know mine," I respond. "Everyone knows who you are. You are one of Baltimore's notorious hitters & dope boys. I'm surprised you ain't get popped sooner."

I know the tension is getting deeper & darker. We have not checked the basketball, nor bounced it. We just size one another up & explore the others defining facial features.

I know in Rell's mind he is probably thinking, "yo just a kid." But nonetheless, "Imma blow this nigga away."

"Nah what I do know is you had beef with him. Who didn't? Everyone had beef with Whoo. What I want to know is why you put me in it? I mean I figured you robbed me, you the only one who could have possibly had my keys. What you failed to do was realize that I have an abundance of resources, & the streets at my disposal." Rell boasts.

"Well what you tryin' do? God please don't let him call my bluff.

"You robbed me, shot me, & framed me. I told you when I catch you, I was going to murder you slim. "

Rell lands a hard hit on my face, bruising my left eye socket. The pain is excruciating, everything just collapsed from there.

Skurrrrrrrrrrr

"Lookout!!

The all-black Chevy Impala darts out the alley into the alley adjacent to the court. Rell Ducks down & the doors swing open.

Brrrrrrr Brrrrr Brrrrr

They spit so many rounds into the concrete wall that lines the sideline of the court.
I limp away & try to get to Marlon but it's too late he takes a few in his arms & legs.
My mom runs out of the house after seeing us in the crossfire & runs behind the concrete pulling Marlon over it. Debris, dust, smoke are flying everywhere. The only action I could do is cover my eye.

 I am ducked over the wall & cannot stop myself from sobbing. I have to man up.
Paul runs around the corner shooting from behind the concrete hitting Rell as he gets up & sprints towards the car. Paul never lets up. He

keeps shooting catching Rell in his face as he turns around to see the carnage & victims. Rell takes a barrage of bullets to the face, ripping through his cheek.

I know I shouldn't but thank God for Paul.
There is smoke in the foreground with sirens in the distance. I messed up.
Big time. Paul checks on us & then sprints off into the distance to hide the evidence.

In Moodah's car they celebrate.

"We burned them niggaz up didn't we Smitty?" Moodah brags.

"Hell yea!" Smitty agrees. "Tell em Rell, fuck around & get smoked!"

"Yo, yo, Rell not moving!" Toya screams. "Yo wake up bruh. Wake up! Oh shit he dead yo! Man they killed my nigga Rell!"

"Damn Rell the fuck! We're going have to ditch him yo!" Smitty panics.

"We're not just throwing my man nowhere!" Replies Moodah.

"Wtf you want us to do Moodah? The nigga is fucking dead. Fuck this car, fuck the body, we gotta survive my nigga." Replies Toya.

"We talking bout Rell here! The nigga would do the same to us if he was still kicking. Fuck this shit and fuck him. I'm with Toya on this one bruh." Smitty reiterates.

"We going wait until the night & take him to the dump by Moravia. It's too fucking hot, fuck!" Moodah complains.

------Back on the court

There are at least 16 police officers. Or maybe it is 8 & me getting punched in the eye has me seeing double. Paramedics attempt to save a few lives of some innocent bystanders that live in section 8 housing buildings who happened to be sitting in lawn chairs enjoying the weather. Imagine getting up & deciding it's too nice to sit in the house, & then being shot in the side of the head.

That's good Shakespearean.

"This one's not going to make it."

"Call it in."

"Get him in the ambulance."

This feeling once again. Why must this cloud of destruction continue to follow me? I absolve myself from this hood shit. I absolve myself from God!

"....Fuck all that, is my brova ok?!"

Trenches

Consequences of Chaos

Terrible decisions breed unnecessary consequences.
I am lounging around in a hospital bed. My leg is in a cast
& sling hanging from the bed rails. Hospital staff says my
leg did not break from the bullets, but when I tried to dash & get over
the wall, the pressure from me pushing off on that leg snapped the
bone separating it. Turns out I was only shot once in the thigh. I won't
be walking for months.
Detective Latham visits me, his familiar suspect.

"Mr. Rob, how are you?"

"Not great but I could be worst. What questions you have for me? You
want a motive? Names? I've got it all!" I joke.

"What's your beef with Terrell?"

"Who? You mean Rell?"

"Yes, him, what is your relationship with him?"

I am a great liar. I can lie on my death bed.

"Oh we had beef because we bet on a dice game down by the
elementary school. Uhm, Bernard Harris. We were shooting & yo felt
like I wasn't supposed to win & said he was going fuck me up."

"That's why he shot at you & Marlon over dice? Seems more personal than that don't you think?"

"As far as I know yea & it's always personal in the hood. It's a jungle out here that's why it's so easy for the cops to do what they do. I don't know much about him or his peep. We were betting big money on the dice game so maybe that was why he was heated I don't know."

I do not know the slightest about shooting dice. I have never ever participated. In fact, I always sat around to watch Rico shoot, & when he did shoot, I could never follow. I am a geek. I play chess, Yugioh, Pokémon. I can tell you anything about those games. The only thing I ever observed was that it was never big money. 1s, 5s & maybe 10s. Never 20s, 50s, or 100s.

"Hmm, where do you get the big money to even bet on dice? You don't work, & don't get a kickback check since you are no longer enrolled. Doesn't sound right but I guess I have to take your word on this too huh?"

"Guess so," I reply.
I know deep down Latham is looking out for me. It's my spark, the same spark that made people on 1300 despise me. They have an aversion for guys like Marlon & I, well at least they used to. But this time it is to my benefit because I should be investigated thoroughly.

"Oh, & you have a young lady waiting in the hallway for you. Let her in."

Detective Latham motions for the officer standing on post at the outside of the door to allow my visitor to come in.

"Hey how you doing kiddo?" Asks Dachel.

I smile bright & wide. "I'm maintaining how have you been? It's been forever."

I have not seen Dachel in a very long time. I cannot calculate the number of months that it has been since that day I exited her life after expressing my regret for killing Rico.

"I'm great been blessed. Finally got that raise I been bugging Mr. Truman for."

Mr. Truman is one of the partners that Dachel works for. She always tells me if I got into a jam, she will put in a word for me & Mr. Truman will take up my case at a lower rate than he would normally charge. Besides I think he has a crush on Dachel.

She always told me stories about how he would liken her to his late wife when she was younger. His attempts at flattery were less than forward but still it takes another man to read the hieroglyphics of the male compliment & analyze it as such.

"That's awesome, you sharing with me? Maybe we can get a carpet in the house." I suggest.

Her visage and body language are obvious & very telling.

"Robby I'm pregnant."

"Wow when was the last..."

"It's not yours. I've been seeing someone for a while now. I met him one day he visited our office seeking legal advice. We hit it off ever since."

"So why are you here Dachel?" I reply. " The nasty pitch in my voice reveals my jealousy & resentment.

"I forgive you for what you told me about my cousin. But I can no longer move forward with you. We're not in love. It's purely physical passion. I've always felt this way. But not about him. I'm moving out. Way away from this place. I'm living with him in his house in the county. I'm tired of living in a place filled with pain. I don't want to raise a child here. Everything here reminds me of you, Rico, death, drugs, Whoo & it's not a healthy environment psychologically for me to attempt to bear a child."

"He sounds like a great man. Sounds like you are ready to get out of the trenches, I can be sad, angry, & feel abandoned, but I can't knock you for overcoming this environment. I-I wish the best for you guys."

She kisses me on the forehead & let's go of my hand that she had been gripping then departs. I let my pride stop me from pursuing her, but from her own admission, dating me is detrimental to her life. The sad thing is I agree.

The emotion from that conversation developed into a headache. All the pain I have endured, & yet I still have learned nothing. I mean of course I knew that things were going to get ugly, but not this ugly. The neighborhood loved me, but God did not. At least that is my fresh new mindset.

Fuck it! Whatever! Who needs God....& who the hell needs Dachel?! I don't need any bitch to make me feel special.

Ring ring!!!

The hospital phone rings it's shordy from McDonald's.

"Hey stranger."

Trenches

Will that Complete Your Order?

"**V**anessa hey I recognize that voice anywhere. How'd you get a hold of me?"

I am mentally compromised, & emotionally perturbed. For 1, Dachel has defecated on my heart which I still have not fully processed. Number 2, I never gave Vanessa my number at McDonald's, so I am a bit disturbed. I have gone to McDonald's plenty times after our first encounter just to flirt & become familiar, but I still was too passive. I never asked for her number, or even to take her out rather.

"Well if you must know, your name is in the newspapers & before your sarcastic behind says anything, yes I read newspapers. Honestly one of my co-workers recognized you from visiting here & told me that the media put a picture of you & your bro on the news. So I followed the paper, put 2&2 together. I saw that you 2 were taken to Mercy medical center so I called around to check on you, & let me tell you, it was not easy. I have been calling up there for at least 3days. Honestly, I was about to stop.

"Well I'm glad you didn't cause it's nice to have someone who isn't a family member care about you," I replied blushing.

"I remember you saying you lived down the street from here. Off of north avenue. So I put my detective skills to work. I was a bit worried about you & wanted to make sure my favorite customer was alright."

"Oh really. A bit stalkerish don't you think?" I joke.

"Don't play with my character. You are not all that for me to be stalking." Vanessa laughs.

What a breath of fresh air it is to converse with someone on the outside of my world who could make judgments & assumptions about me but didn't. I cannot talk to Marlon because he is in an induced coma after the surgery.

The surgeon says he was only shot twice, & my first thought was, "doc you weren't there." The surgeon says there is a single bullet that ricocheted from Marlon's arm to his lung which punctured it. They managed to patch it up, but he still cannot breathe on his own which is why he has to remain "sleep".

The other bullet grazed his collar bone. I assume that is why he flailed as much, trying to dodge the gunfire. It was pointless seeing as he was a big red target pinned between a concrete wall & 4 shooters. They were amateurs though. Rell's people hit everything except Marlon & I. But if our mom had not pulled him over the wall, there might have been an autopsy report instead.

"But on the serious note how are you holding up Hun?" Vanessa asks.

"Physically I'm devastated and psychologically I'm even more fucked up," I reply. "Excuse my language it's just been that kind of week."

"Boy please we are adults here."

I break the awkward silence with a laugh & ask Vanessa, "don't take this the wrong way, but do you want to work at McDonald's forever?"

"Of course this is my dream job, I love taking orders!" ...... "the fuck?! Of course not. I'm in school McDonald's is just a means to money. It's one of the reasons I read newspapers, to get information on better jobs & interesting events that are happening around Baltimore."

"See I thought I was going to have to stop talking to you. Pretty girls always have that smart-ass mouth." I snicker.

"So I'm pretty now huh? Well Don't think you getting a compliment."

"Chill on me. Just be glad I gave you one. I don't know what Imma do with your mouth. Is your hair still the same color?"

"Nope see if you paid me a visit you would know. It's black again. Yep, my natural color."

"Ok guess Imma have to see it for myself. When will that be?"

"When do you want it to be?" Vanessa quips.

"Well how about whenever you are free, you visit me here. We can watch TV & chop it up for a few...if your comfortable seeing me mummified. I'm all wrapped up."

"Anything else while I'm tending to your every need?" Vanessa jokes.

"Well now that you mentioned it, this hospital food is terrible so let me get a number 8....whatever that is."

"You a trip lil erky ass. I got you."

"Preciate it loves. When you come up, we can kick it on the humble. I kind of want to pick your brain some more."

"I'd like that..."

Our first date in a hospital...how original.

"Knock knock. Mr. Peters. I'm Dr. Ursula. Your brother is being pulled from the machine & should be waking up. Do you want to be there to see him?"

"Does a dog chase its tail? Of course."

Trenches

Tears of our past

Snap...Snap

"Marlon are you with us? Nurse Harris keeps the crash cart outside on standby just in case he codes." Dr. Ursula orders.

Some kid working for the hospital wheels me in. I feel out of sync having someone be my mobility, it is not a great feeling.

"Why are you here?" Robert Sr. Asks.

"Why else?! Not for you! I'm here for my brother. Which is more than what I can say for you? I don't want your pity. We all know Marlon is your favorite! The son that never fucked up, the son that's going somewhere!"

"At least he's doing something with himself!" Robert Sr. argues.

"Did you ever think that if you were around or interacted with your firstborn son that maybe I could have been on a path that you accepted!?"

We barely talk, it is like we tiptoed around each other when we are both home. Most of the time when he is home, I would make it my job to not be.

Our history is one of such disdain, which only makes us anti-social around each other for the most part. We speak the bare minimum on the days where we can coexist.

"That's enough!" Angie shouts. "Right now you need to get yourself in order & you need to get yourself in order." She points.

"Right now we should just be thankful that both of our sons are alive. Don't forget you were locked up, & you were selling drugs when you were his age so don't condemn him. Teach him better."

Angie is not taking sides, or speaking on who is right or wrong, but about peace. If there exists no peace amid chaos, then what will be solved?

"So when should we expect him to wake up doc?" I finally ask.

"Well he's breathing on his own which is a good sign. He's young, healthy, athletic so he may recover faster. We're expecting him to wake within the hour."

"Thank you." Robert Sr. Replies. "And please forgive us for being less than civil earlier. Every family has their crosses to bear, we need to put ours aside...for Marlon."

My deep dark brown eyes meet my dad's eyes & I wheel myself out of the room. I get back to the elevator, pressing the up button to leave the surgery floor when Angie stops me.

"You ok Hun?" She asks.

"Yea mom I'm........"

"Don't yea me!"

"Yes mom I'm fine. Just going go back to my room & take a nap, my homegirl is supposed to be coming to see me."

"Oh you want mama to wash you up while she's there?"

"Ma what kind of question is that?! You trying to embarrass me?" We both laugh.

"Alright I'll check on you before we leave, we're going to spend some time with Marlon until we hear progress," Angie explains.

"Ok love you."

"Love you too Robby...I'm proud of you."

That struck a nerve, the elevator comes just in time as I tear up. I start sobbing as the doors close. I avoid pressing a floor number to gain my composure before those doors reopened & everyone saw me for the scared half a man I am.

Back in my room I get to the bed to press the call button for a nurse. Nurse Gina comes in & gets my body situated. I turn on the news to channel Fox 45 at 5:00 pm & watch the developing story.
****

"That's right Phil we don't know what took place almost a week ago. Police have speculated that rival gang members or rival neighborhood members had an altercation that ended deadly. The alleged suspect 28-year-old Terrell Jenkins was found dead in a garbage bin in the dump on Moravia road. He was arrested just months ago for a fatal death on 32-year-old Whoo also known as Donte Brown. There are at least 4 other shooters at large, & no one in the community is saying anything."
****

"Wooooow," I say silently to myself. "No wonder there are guards stationed outside my room." I believe that this is the last night they will be here. They can retire this armed security it is not like I'm Justin Bieber or someone.
A few hours past & Angie comes up to say goodnight.

"Any word on Marlon?" I ask.

"He's not awake yet, and it's been 3 hours so we're going home we have to work, but the doctor said that if he's not up then they are going to have to rush him back into emergency surgery to see what's what. Your sisters are supposed to be coming into town, but they didn't give me a definite time."

"Ok mom get some sleep, I might go sit with him for a while. Love you."

"Love you too night."

Sigh... "Nurse Gina?!"

Trenches

Resentment

"Thanx nurse Gina."

"You're welcome dear," Gina replies as she walks back to her floor to check on her other patients.

"Damn Marlon." I begin to speak as I close the door. "I didn't want any of this for you, for us. I'm the older brother I'm supposed to be the moral one. I'm sorry for fucking up your future."

I look away from his body to hide my tears. The very lives that a lot of us young black guys living in the city of Baltimore ends with death, despair, or jail. I do not envision myself going anywhere after this.

I remember back when I was fresh out of high school, & I decided to go to Immaculata University in Pennsylvania. It was a chance of a lifetime. They offered everything except room & board. Everything was covered except for my living situation.

"Dad they just sent a letter saying they need $250 now before I go, & another $250 at the end of summer to cover dorm costs." I read to him from the outside of the bathroom door.

"Ok son, I'll send it up. Do me a favor, bring me a roll of toilet paper." Robert Sr. replies.

Later down the line as it got closer to the time school starts back up, I realize I had to constantly remind him that I need him to mail the money.

A week later...

"Hey, mom did he send the money up yet?" I ask.

"I don't know, you have to ask him. Stay on him about it." Angie replies.

Months later.......

"Dad did you send the...."

"Yes Robert I sent them $250 up 2 weeks ago! I'm sending the rest tomorrow. Leave me alone!"

That entire time he did not even know I have the letter from Immaculata stating that I would not be admitted to the university because I did not present the funds to live on campus. From that day on, I held a disdain for him.

In my eyes my future is gone, & he never brought it up. Never asked about school, never asked about anything except "Are you looking for a job?"

That is where our friction began, & ultimately is still thriving on. I had to put myself in college after he would not bother to care about me. I was his practice son.... & he was going to get it right the second time around.

"It's no secret that I've always been jealous & envious of you Marlon. You're the younger brother, but you make my parents happier & prouder than I ever could. It would take no effort for me to put this pillow over your face & watch you turn blue."

I am immediately frightened by my own words! Even in his death I will find no comfort nor acceptance from my father.

"But you are my brother, I love you no matter how much I hate myself. You are the gift this family needs. So I need you to wake up to keep being that little brother that I can look up to! I need you to get out of Baltimore to live. I need you to open your eyes!"

Nurse Harris comes in & begins prepping him.

"What's going on?" I ask.

"Well we waited long enough I'm taking him to the OR so they can prep him for surgery."

She moves the bed & starts out the door with help from a tech. As soon as his head is out of the threshold of the door, Marlon's hand grabs the frame.

With one eye open he says, "Jealousy is a female trait", & proceeds to fall back into his unconsciousness.

Trenches

Jury of my Peers.... Guilty thoughts

"We initially figured his condition was due to being shot, but it is more so the aftermath of being shot. He hit his head on the concrete sustaining damage to the lower cranial region." Neurosurgeon Dr. Tyler explains.

"So what does that mean?" Tiffany asks. Tiffany is my oldest sister. We share the same mother but separate fathers. She lives out of state in North Carolina with her husband. She arrived while Marlon was in surgery.

"It means that he has fluid on his brain. He can send the signal to breathe on his own recently but is constantly falling in & out of consciousness."

"So you guys fixed the problem?" Angie asks.

"Well for now he's stable, as long as he continues breathing on his own, he will be fine. We removed plenty of fluid. His head is still swollen but otherwise he's not in immediate life-threatening danger. We're still going to monitor him closely for a while."

"Well I guess any news is good news," I reply.

"Whatsup Robby?" Tiffany greets.

"Nada, same old same old, trying to stay out of trouble."

"And what a poor job of executing ." Tiffany quips.

"Fuck you, stuck up prick", I said to myself as I cut my eyes in her direction.

"Cut it out Tiff. Right now Marlon needs all positive energy to find his strength."

This is all my fault. Tiff is right in her assumption of me causing all of this unnecessary trouble. How can anyone be strong while in a coma? It is a tough pill to swallow, I mean it should be me laying here soaked in my sweat & blood, wrapped in bandages.

Maybe my dad is correct in his lack of compassion & love for me. Maybe his trivial opinion of me is warranted and necessary. Maybe I am a bad son but cannot see it.

I may be projecting only one side of my dad, but it is my story, I have to tell it however I feel necessary.

"Tiff bite me. Then take your ass back down south where you came." I holler.

The whole point in the family coming together is to be a unit, not to reject one another and place blame. It is always different sides of the family bickering over nothing instead of combining our efforts & resources.

It makes no difference to me because it is just a matter of time before I am discharged & can find somewhere else to live away from Lafayette & my family. I found interest in a girl & started to feel human again. Vanessa is that redemption that allows me to hopefully in time finally adjust my life.

I do not know what it is, but that girl makes me feel important, special even, but I have to make sure not to get ahead of myself.

I feel regular in the sense that I will be free of hood issues like guns, murder, drugs, & the police. Well I will always have to duck the police because I am black. Plus I am a male. A black male is a target....an endangered species even.

I feel like Pink Floyd, another brick in the wall. That wall is full of the same black men that are cut from the cloth of underprivileged lives & poverty.

"Can y'all stop fussing for one moment and let a brother get some sleep?" Marlon asks.

"About time you stopped napping." Tiff jokes.

"Knock. knock hey everyone!" Erica greets.

"Hey baby." Angie hugs.

Erica, my other sister is a bit freer spirited & less of a nuisance than Tiff. She is my father's favorite. She lives in Ocean City Maryland with her significant other & 2 kids.
The gang is all here, except Robert Sr. he is at work of course but I am sure he will be here shortly to make it known that he loves Erica the most.

"Hey Erica, hey Tiff. I feel like it's been a long time since the family was together. Dad's at work?" Marlon asks.

"Yes he will be here shortly. It looks like you are getting back to normal. Well I'm staying the night and your father probably stays as well if you guys wanna get some shuteye." Says Angie.

"Cool since all of you are here, I am going back to my room, they should be removing the casts in the morning. I have a date!"

"In the hospital? How corny & cliché you damn nerd!" Erica replies.

"Ha very funny smidget. I'll see y'all tomorrow."

It feels great seeing my immediate family, even though that joy is overshadowed by the echo of Marlon's haunting voice telling me he heard everything I said.

I will wash these sins away when I get to my room, then hit the chapel for 5 more Hail Mary's.

Man...I might be going to hell.

Trenches

Do you want Your Receipt?

Gina is back again this morning to put up with, as she says it, "pain in the behind" & removes this cast from my leg. I get it removed early because I have been exercising a lot more without assistance. Way more mobility from here on out.

Things are turning around as my brother is getting nursed back to health. My family is altogether which they have not been for years, even before my descent into this chaos.

I worry that as soon as I think things are turning around, God or the devil tosses a wrench in the mix, & I scrap for my humanity.

I'm still anticipating Vanessa's arrival like a shark stalking its prey. I check the time periodically, check the phones to make sure they work, & keep glancing at the door anxious for her face.

Ring Ring

"Hey Robby, we are going to have prayer service in the chapel later on tonight so don't be too busy with that little girlfriend of yours." Tiff berates.

"Whatever, make sure your husband not sneaking around with his side-chick!" I reply as I hang the phone up on the hook. My eyes dash to the door as Gina smiles at me.

"Mr. Peters you have a guest," Gina says most graciously as possible.

"She can come in. Don't act nice now nurse Gina." I joke.

We both share a laugh as Vanessa comes through the entrance & pulls up a chair right next to my bed.

"What's up erky?" She greets.

"Hey whatsup, give me a hug fry cook." I quip back.

"Oh you got jokes huh? You must want me to request a male nurse to give you a sponge bath huh?"

I laugh, "don't do that! Besides that's what I have you for."

"I'm not touching your funky butt boy!"

"It's not funky! Anyways what's up? When do you go back to work?"

"Well I go back next week; I took the week off because my friend has been hospitalized for being young & reckless."

"Oh just a friend huh?" I reply.

"Boy is that all you got out of what I said? For real though I want you to get a real job making real money, as a matter of fact, scratch that. I want you to go back to school. Money can wait."

Vanessa stands up to pull her pants up a bit. She is beautiful, not a bad bitch, not a sexy woman, but beautiful. I can imagine queens of Egypt which she resembles in all of her radiant melanin.
Her caramel skin & slender waist is to die for. In my mind I thought, "Dachel who?" She is enough for me & will always be enough as long as I didn't do anything stupid to lose her.

"Umma try love. Trust me. It is a process. With everything happening to me & around me....you can't imagine how much time I have had to reflect."

"It sounds like you are making an excuse. I'm not going to trust you if you will only try. My future baby daddy needs to have education & goals planned, not street cred & a criminal background."

She is getting ahead of herself, but I love every bit of it. I need it. A smart girl, scratch that, a smart woman to shake me out of this combined assault of worthlessness & self-loathing.

"You are 1000% right Vanessa. Since my issues with my father not doing what he should have education-wise, I never appreciated myself & I never fully applied myself. But after this incident with my brother, I'm not going to be included of this type of life. I promise you that."

"Great, so this should not be an issue down the line correct? By the way, what are we watching?" Vanessa replies.

"Uhm SpongeBob. And please don't judge. If this wasn't on, it would have been some other cartoon."

"You a big ass kid huh? Damn shame, but uhm is this the episode that SpongeBob gets his license?" Vanessa asks.

I look at her, "& you calling me a damn big kid.? Nah see I can't take you already."

"You knew! So are you getting discharged today?"

"Yea I should be. My leg is pretty much in good shape, still has gauze on it no more casts or slings so I should be fine. Later on I'm going downstairs to the chapel where my family is meeting with the pastors or whoever they hire here & we're going to pray. You can either stay up here until I'm finished, or you can come down and hang for a few. I don't want you feeling uncomfortable."

"Boy please. Oh so I get to meet your family on the first date? I must be special."

"Yep you special alright, that's the only way you got that job at Micky Dees." I holler.

"Your too much I don't know if I can handle your smart mouth erky. But umma time up for that ass eventually."

Vanessa slides her nice pretty sandals off of her pretty cinnamon colored feet. Her toenails are a lime green hue & glossy as if she has them done for a specific occasion.
She then makes her way to the bed & slides my arm under her, making this innocent face as she rubs my wound on my leg gently.

I pull the sheets over the top of her, kiss her hair, & turn the volume up. As awkward as this encounter seemed to be, it is amazing & fluid. I can tell she has prepared & anticipated this day for a while. So have I. The simple connection in my mind is nothing but wanting to know more about her rather than just mount her like another nigga. She is more than just a piece of ass, but an amalgamation of emotions, experiences & mystery that held my attention.

Hearing SpongeBob laugh has Gina snickering in the hallway. She peeps her head in & smiles warmly as if she knew I needed this "win".

I look back into the doorway & notice my dad, mom & sisters observe me silently. Angie & Robert both are smiling at our embrace. Tiffany & Erica are making faces of disgust, typical sisters. They exit as stealthily as they had arrived in order not to disturb us.

"Today would be perfect if only...."

"If only what?" Vanessa asks dumbfounded.

"If only you had brought my burgers!" I laugh.

"Boy, hush, you are ruining my drool session."

Trenches

Reconciliation

Vanessa & I are the last to arrive at the chapel. She has been with me the entire day. The nurse for the night Kelly has brings me down in a wheelchair with all of my belongings & discharge papers.

As Kelly opens the chapel doors, Vanessa & I walk arm to arm locked. I leave the wheelchair in the hallway. Every eye is fixated on us, & there is nothing but divine smells filling the room. To me, this image is a bit of a foreshadow, at least, I hope. Vanessa & I walk through a church, wedding bells & everyone else waiting for us.

Marlon sits in a wheelchair closest to my Robert Sr. When I get into arms reach, Marlon nudges me & attempts to hold back his perverted grin. The audacity Marlon has in checking Vanessa out has me with conflicting emotions. I don't know whether to punch him or dap him up.

"Should have been me. I was going to order from her register if that black spook lady didn't open up first." Marlon says as he daps me up. "She looks even better out of her uniform hombre."

"She's pretty Robby," Angie says. "Hi how are you honey I'm Angie, Robert's mother. That's his dad, brother & 2 sisters."

"Nice to meet you all. And Miss Angie your hair is lovely."

"Oh thank you girl, after this when you come to the house, I'll hook you up with my stylist's number." Says Angie as she runs her fingers through her bob.

"Thank you I appreciate it," Vanessa replies.

"Look at you, already trying to get in good with moms." I snicker.

"Have to let her know you are mine now. I got this from here on out." Vanessa whispers.

"Are we finally ready to proceed?" Asks the minister.

"Yes, yes everyone is here now." Replies Robert Sr.

"Ok let us begin. Everyone hold hands. *Father we come here asking that you bless this family. Each individual in his & her way. We ask that you give them health as they journey through and through. We ask that you protect them from every choice they may make. Be it life lessons or bad decisions. And let them not fall by the waist side. Let them not collapse under the pressure of Satan & his emissaries but continue to allow them to choose their paths & create their futures. In your blessed name, Amen.*"

After the prayer that seems conveniently directed towards me ends, Tiffany, Erica & Vanessa begin getting acquainted. Marlon, his nurse

& Angie also converse. The aura shifts when Robert Sr. opens his mouth.

"Junior, walk me to the vending machine."

My dad has not called me junior in years. Junior is a sign of respect. It is like making others aware that I am his offspring which has not been done for what seems like centuries. Angie, Marlon, Tiffany & Erica momentarily cease their conversations as they catch the new events unfolding.

We walk around the corners of the extremely well-lit hospital towards the visitor's area.
"I know we have a bad history. And I know my choices are the root of a lot of our demons, but son, I'm proud of you....regardless."

I quickly turn my head to fight back the tears. I cannot let pops see me cry.

"I'm even more proud of you for that little young tender you have."

"Ha-ha yea she is something else, isn't she?" I reply while wiping away my eye drippings.
I step up in front of the vending machine, insert my dollar, & press A25.

Clink

A large butterfingers candy bar plummets to the bottom. We reconvene with the rest of the family with a newfound respect for one another. I relinquish all hate & animosity towards him. I am still a bit standoffish because I wonder, "where do we go from here?", but it is not the same objective disposition that we are both accustomed to.

I brush that curiosity under the thought of, "what secrets did they give Vanessa? She is quick on her feet & the last thing she needs is more ammunition!" I have to hurry back before everyone destroys what little positive reputation I have left.

We regroup with everyone. We walk while my dad simultaneously holds my shoulder as a father should as we smile still conversing in our imperfect bubble. The entire room warms with this ever-present light. I am in the best mood I have been in the past few days. I even want to share my sweets.

"Want to split this candy bar?" I ask Vanessa.

"Split? Boy that's my favorite candy, you going to have to come off that, especially if you want a ride home." Vanessa baits. I hand her the unopened, probably most delicious candy bar that I had to limp, sweat & fight for. "Good choice, I have a sweet tooth." Vanessa celebrates.

"You drive too?! Lord you can have it all!" I exclaim, which awarded me a negative eyebrow raise from the minister & my mom.

"Don't use his name in vain Robby!" Angie scolds.

"Yea, yea blah blah it was a mistake," I mutter. "I guess we can get outta here now so you can be back in the house before 11:00. The last thing I want is your peep thinking I'm more irresponsible than I am."

"Yea, yea, it was nice meeting all of you. Marlon, get well soon."

"Goodnight, I'll get up with you all tomorrow," I reply.

Exiting with Vanessa makes things clearer. My decisions are becoming more coherent. That negative energy just needed to be expelled from my being. Tired of my life being a cliff hanger.

Trenches

Now Why You Going Do That?

Buggy has been pestering everyone about the basketball court incident ever since it happened. He tries to convince Hammond, C.J, Freaky, & Paul to retaliate, but they do not want any parts of it. I have been in contact with Paul ever since I was admitted to the hospital.

I told Paul," don't let anyone come up here man, I don't need y'all feeling bad for me, keep living. More importantly live positive."

"Rob you know we were going come up with some balloon, flowers, & fuck up your cred." Paul jokes.

"Nigga you stupid. Aye have any detectives or police approached you or the rest of the fellas?" I ask.

"Yea during the first couple days when it happened & after it, they were asking the entire neighborhood you feel me. Why have they specifically said anything about any of us?

"Nah, nah, well they haven't asked anything about anyone for real. I'm assuming they are looking into the other shooters he had with him. Maybe they are treating this investigation a bit differently. Rell was murdered but they don't know by who."

"Yea that could be a possibility, but I'm still going to tell everyone to lay low & keep off the streets. Oh & make sure you talk to Buggy man, you have to."

"He has hatred in his heart, what makes you think he going to listen to me?" I reply raising one eyebrow.

"You know he looks up to you, don't even front. Shit, he has no siblings, no dad. It's just his mom & she works all of the time. Just make sure you talk to him before he directs his anger in the wrong vicinity."

I am a mentor in some sense to Buggy, I do not understand why. I am not a positive example of a big brother which is evident by the recent events.

"Another thing Rob, I asked around & get this, the first time Rell was so close to finding you were cause he asked around. Guess who he asked. George!"

"How the fuck George & him sit down and converse about me?" I ask confused.

"George be everywhere. Junkies don't get tired man. George be down the hill too, scoping out homes." Paul explains.

"Damn."

"The second time guess who. It was from. John."

"What the fuck?! And I gave that nigga some food. Well fuck it. God bless them. I'm not holding on to it." I reply.

Buggy knows that George & John are both involved. He is so heated which is the reason he wants to get the fellas involved with the payback. But like I said, they are not having that.

"Good!"

....

"Man Hammond get me a Glock." Buggy pleads.

"Man nobody going to give your crazy lead paint ass no damn burner," C.J exclaims.

"Besides that, look how heavy it is round here. All these pigs shit I wouldn't be surprised if they put a surveillance light up." Hammond says.

"So I'm the only person that goes hard? Y'all some pussies. I'm out." Buggy yells.

He proceeds to get back on his bike to ride around the block in frustration. It's dead outside, & Buggy finds himself bored of popping wheelies, so he decides to explore the busier side across Hartford road.

BUGGY'S POINT OF VIEW

"Damn, hella drug transactions, niggas getting money over here."

I lean my bike to the side, squeezing the brakes, & step off the pedal as I observe each face. Some familiar, more unfamiliar.

As I ride past an alley, I see a very familiar face. "Look at John bitch ass" I thought. Time to confront him.

"Ay John what's up? Let me rap to you for a min." I holler.

"Whaddup shordy?" John greets.

"Nada, trying to flip these packs, you want in?"

"Get the fuck outta here before I rob ya ass. Fucking turkey!

I was heated, "I ain't no turkey, don't disrespect me." John starts to walk away.

I run up on John from behind, dropping my bike handle, open my switchblade & ram it in the middle of his spine.

"Who's a turkey now? Fucking junkie!" I scream as I spit in his direction.

After John's initial scream, he grows eerily quiet. He starts foaming & his legs convulse violently. John's eyes are a milky yellow & grow a mustard yellow the more he twitches.

I am extremely terrified. I hop on my bike & haul ass home. I remove off my sweat-soaked shirt & stash the blade in the tiles in the ceiling. The blood-drenched blade remains in an open position dripping as if ketchup.

The rage goes away, but the fear evolves.

Knock knock a couple of hours later

It's Paul.

"Yo, what the fuck did you do?!"

Trenches

St. Bernard

A few months pass with Marlon being released from Johns Hopkins hospital after he is examined by the brain surgeon. He is healthy, no motor skill degeneration, & no neurological damage.

Vanessa drives me around to Paul's crib. I know he lives close, but I want to stunt & show off Vanessa to him.

"That's you Rob?" Paul asks with a grin.

"Been, been," I reply dapping him up. "Paul this is Vanessa. Vanessa, this is Paul."

"Nice to finally meet you sis." Paul greets as he shakes my lady's hand.

"And you as well," Vanessa replies with that genuine McDonald's employee.

"So what's up what did you want to meet up for?"

"You have your piece?" I ask.

"Yea what I need my gun for? Don't tell me we have more beef because if it is anything like what we went through, then I don't want to live this lifestyle bruh. I don't mean to leave you on your own, but I can't do that anymore. After letting Buggy see all of the shit we have participated in, I can't be a role model to that." Paul explains.

"I know, I know, just trust me. That is why I'm bringing Buggy along. He must come along. Listen it's one last heist." I joke.

"Heist huh?"

"Just get your gun, we have to scoop Marlon, & Buggy then make our way."
Earlier that day I ask Vanessa, "do you mind if I go to my exes to grab something?"

"As long as I'm rolling with you. Just don't do nothing I wouldn't."
Vanessa quips.

"Now you know that's not happening. I already called her & asked if her husband wouldn't mind me stopping pass their house to get something in remembrance of my late friend." I explain.

"That's fine like I said, as long as I'm riding with you."

"Well duh, who else is going to chauffeur me?" I laugh.

Vanessa touches her index finger to her thumb & plucks my earlobe as she is accustomed to. You can imagine because of my mouth; I get plucked often.

We gather everyone up that I deem necessary because not everyone can fit in Vanessa's Pontiac. Vanessa's in the driver's seat of course. Buggy, Paul, & Marlon are in the back seats while I occupy the passenger seat.

It is around midnight when we arrive at Fells point. Fells point is an area near the water that hosts a variety of different bars & eateries. It is a diverse area located on the edge of downtown Baltimore. We plan to go late so that we will look inconspicuous.

We park in the projects then walk down Broadway's long strip & arrive at the water. I prepare a speech but did not recite any of it. I just speak from the heart.

"I do not have all the answers, the cards in life have never been dealt in my favor, but what I do know is that there are others out there that have a worst hand than I. Buggy, there's more than what you have witnessed in the streets. Marlon can attest to that. So can Paul & Vanessa. They have seen greater things than I have. We will be an example that we should have been. Hell, look at me. My little brother is the one who is an inspiration to me."

I take my gun from my waist & toss it into the water. I take the photo of Rico along with his lighter & burn it.

"To my man Rico, we both have made unwise decisions. I forgive you as I ask for you to forgive me."

"To new beginnings," Paul says as he drops his piece in the water. Buggy tosses his blade in the water & closes his eyes as he remembers John. John died after complications of pneumonia after being paralyzed by the trauma to his spine.
Vanessa embraces my words with a kiss. She sees the guy I was before hell broke loose on Lafayette.

I turn to Marlon. "You probably cannot remember what I said in the hospital, & I am happy about your amnesia. Just know I'm sorry for it all man. I am prepared to live a peaceful, drama-free life. I'm prepared to set new goals instead."

"You have come a long way. And I may not remember what you said, but that's because it is behind us." Marlon states. "I'm proud of you Rob, & Rico would be too."
"That was a good thing you did Robby. Buggy needs that realization, & it should have only come from you." Vanessa whispers.

"I hope so love, I will embody the spirit of a brother to Buggy. I plan on enrolling back in school & staying away from trouble." I reply.

"By the way Buggy what is your real name?" Paul inquires. " We been knowing him forever & niggaz always just call you Buggy with your beady eyes.

"Bernard." Buggy replies.
Bernard...I can get used to that.

The end.
Trenches

Made in the USA
San Bernardino, CA
13 July 2020